He'd just found out the truth, and now it might be too late to make things right…

Garrett nodded as he pushed open the door at the top of the stairs into daylight. The rest of the building was gone. Nothing but the head frame and smelter remained. He could see the administration building had sustained some damage but remained standing. People started coming out of their hiding places, some looking shell shocked, others with a few scratches.

"You!" Garrett waved to several able-bodied miners as he stumbled over debris. He pointed to different locations. "Start searching for people trapped. Charleston," he yelled, spotting the man walking around in a daze. "Wake up! Make sure all your people are either underground or hunkered down. Make sure the generators kicked in." Stunned, Charleston stared at him. Garrett shook him. "Do your job!"

Charleston swallowed hard and nodded before walking off. Garrett's truck had been pelted with hail but remained drivable. Garrett continued to give orders as he slid into the front seat of his truck. In seconds, he was racing through the twisted gates and toward the main street in the town of Westfork. Overturned cars, smashed store fronts, and downed trees were the first thing that he spotted. But it was when he turned down the street where the school was located that he slammed on the brakes.

It was gone.

Returning home in hopes of putting her life back together after several disastrous relationships, Fawn Turnbough finds that the man who drove her away ten years earlier is waiting to pick up where he left off. Her father is determined to keep them apart and hide the secret that forced her to run away from the handsome Garrett Horton. He's convinced Garrett wants Fawn's inheritance and his lead mines. But nothing will stop Garrett this time from taking what he wants most—a heart as hard as the lead he brings up from the Ozark mines.

KUDOS for *The Rescued Heart*

In *The Rescued Heart* by Tierney James, Fawn Turnbough comes back to her hometown of Westfork, Missouri, after ten years and a failed marriage, only to find that the reason she left in the first place is still there—Garrett Horton—and still wants to marry her. But she is convinced that he only wants her so that he can have her father's lead mines. But as she and Garrett take up where they left off, secrets are revealed that shake the very foundations of Fawn's world. James clearly has a vast knowledge of the lives of lead miners and their families and the trials and tribulations of the life they have chosen. From tornados to mine cave-ins, it is not an easy life. But James tells it all in a way that will leave you wanting more. ~ *Taylor Jones, Reviewer*

The Rescued Heart by Tierney James is the heartwarming story of love, courage, hardship, and the grassroots, down and dirty, nitty-gritty way of life of some of the country's hard rock miners. Our heroine Fawn ran away ten years ago after she was betrayed by her fiancé, Garrett. Now she is back and Garrett wants to take up where they left off. Fawn is determined to not to give into him, but her good intentions fall short when Garrett sweeps back into her life and starts courting her in earnest. The story has a ring of truth that is rare for debut authors. Not only are the characters realistic, well-developed, and charming, but the everyday struggles they face are entirely plausible. Either James has "been there and done that" or she did an enormous amount of research. Either way it makes for a touching and poignant story that will tug at your heartstrings. ~ *Regan Murphy, Reviewer*

ACKNOWLEDGEMENTS

I would like to thank the Viburnum, Missouri community for years of friendship and support through the history we've shared together as miners and miners' wives.

The Rescued Heart

By

Tierney James

A Black Opal Books Publication

GENRE: ROMANTIC SUSPENSE/WOMEN'S FICTION

This is a work of fiction. Names, places, characters and incidents are either the product of the author's imagination or are used fictitiously, and any resemblance to any actual persons, living or dead, businesses, organizations, events or locales is entirely coincidental. All trademarks, service marks, registered trademarks, and registered service marks are the property of their respective owners and are used herein for identification purposes only. The publisher does not have any control over or assume any responsibility for author or third-party websites or their contents.

THE RESCUED HEART
Copyright © 2015 by Tierney James
Cover Design by Jackson Cover Designs
All cover art copyright © 2015
All Rights Reserved
Print ISBN: 978-1-626942-43-1

First Publication: MARCH 2015

All rights reserved under the International and Pan-American Copyright Conventions. No part of this book may be reproduced or transmitted in any form or by any means, electronic or mechanical, including photocopying, recording, or by any information storage and retrieval system, without permission in writing from the publisher.

WARNING: The unauthorized reproduction or distribution of this copyrighted work is illegal. Criminal copyright infringement, including infringement without monetary gain, is investigated by the FBI and is punishable by up to 5 years in federal prison and a fine of $250,000.

ABOUT THE PRINT VERSION: If you purchased a print version of this book without a cover, you should be aware that the book is stolen property. It was reported as "unsold and destroyed" to the publisher, and neither the author nor the publisher has received any payment for this "stripped book."

IF YOU FIND AN EBOOK OR PRINT VERSION OF THIS BOOK BEING SOLD OR SHARED ILLEGALLY, PLEASE REPORT IT TO: lpn@blackopalbooks.com

Published by Black Opal Books **http://www.blackopalbooks.com**

DEDICATION

To my husband who taught me everything about mining. And to the hard rock miners everywhere that put their lives on the line to get the lead out.

Chapter 1

A dusty breeze moved across the open yard of gravel and asphalt, causing a ghost-like cloud to rise up from the ground. Fawn shaded her eyes from the late August sun and tightened her lips against the gritty taste forcing its way onto her tongue. With apprehension, she watched the cage rise once more out of the shaft with men leaving the lead mines.

Through the haze Fawn saw him step off the cage and move toward her like a proud lion. His face was black with grime. Not even that could hide the chiseled good looks that had been the cause of many a young girl's surrender. His long legs were firm and sure as they brought him closer. Although his body had thickened with a muscular maturity, he remained agile. The sight of his large hands still astounded her, knowing the gentleness they contained. Those eyes, like blue lasers, slicing through her defenses, as if she were just seventeen and his first virgin, still paralyzed her with a fleeting thought of no escape. But now she was older, stronger, and vowed never to be such a fool for a man, especially this man.

Their eyes locked; not flinching or showing fear as each measured the other's ability to survive. Fawn blinked only when one side of his mouth turned up in a slight smirk. It was then that she noticed her father walking by Garrett's side along with another man.

Upon seeing him, Fawn realized her father, Big Jim Turnbough, began to smile. He stepped a little ahead of the two men. With a wave of his hand, he dismissed them like servants. One split off and headed for the changing room. Garrett Horton, eyes still glued to her face, ignored her aging father just as he always had.

Fawn wondered, again, why her father had never fired such a self-righteous braggart, especially after what he'd done to his only child.

Watching Jim look with intolerance at Garrett was an amusing moment for Fawn. She knew her father wanted the young engineer to mold to his wishes. But hadn't that been why he kept him around all these years? Garrett Horton was a lot of things but he wasn't a "yes" man. He damned near loved the company as much as her father did.

Her father created a great many obstacles those early years between his innocent daughter and the country boy he claimed to despise. She'd forgiven her father. It had seemed like the right thing to do at the time. Her father said he couldn't be sure Garrett wanted his Fawn or the company. Either way, both lives had never been the same without the other. Fawn had gone through a loveless marriage and then an affair with some notorious character from Chicago.

Even while she'd been living in Chicago, rumors had reached her that Garrett was married to his work and loved it passionately. Only recently did he move in with a local beautician and her small son. The whole town knew, much to Fawn's disgust, that Garrett Horton loved only two things: Turnbough Lead Company and the one person who could hand him the keys to the company. Some things never changed.

For a moment, Fawn wondered if the deception from long ago could survive a chance for them to reconcile. She wanted children to carry on the legacy of Turnbough Lead Company and she knew her mother wanted the same.

"Fawn, what brings you out on such a hot day?" Jim wiped the sweat from his face with one hand. It would never occur to him she might be feeling uncomfortable under Garrett's riveting stare. "Come inside, honey, where it's cooler."

"No, Dad, I—" Her gaze slid to Garrett with contempt. She needed to acknowledge him. "Hello, Garrett. You're looking fit." She tried not to sound smug.

Garrett's smirk widened into a smile, revealing straight white teeth. His blue eyes twinkled like a mischievous little boy. "And you, Fawn, are as beautiful as you are sorry to see me."

"It's so refreshing to know someone who can get the message so easily. Then again, you always grasped the obvious."

"When it came to you, Fawn, I'm afraid I had only one thing on my mind." He grinned flippantly, as her father frowned at the insinuation. "See you later, Jim. I need to clean up." His eyes, narrowed against the sun, had not left Fawn's face. He gave her a little salute to his hard hat with one finger then strode off at an easy gait.

Fawn blew her hair from her face. "Oh! He is so full of himself. How could I ever…" Her eyes turned back to her father. She was surprised to see him laughing. "What?"

"You. I haven't seen so much color in your face since you were twelve years old and Garrett came carrying you home with a broken leg. He took full responsibility for your misbehaving so you wouldn't feel my belt."

Fawn didn't want to remember. Those days were gone forever.

The old Garrett Horton no longer existed. He was a tyrant now, just like her father. Garrett would stop at nothing until he had a piece of Turnbough Lead.

She stiffened her resolve. He wouldn't be getting it through her.

"Never mind that." Fawn lifted her hand in dismissal. She, too, had that air of superiority that came with money. "You are to stop by Dr. Tony's office on the way home from work. Mother tried to call you twice but the lines were out again. This god-forsaken place needs to get a cell phone tower. Wasn't that supposed to be in two weeks ago? I swear this town is stuck in the twentieth century. I wouldn't have to come here if you'd get better communications." Fawn sighed. "She'll meet you there at five. Daddy. Please don't be late this time. You have plenty of people to pick up the slack." Fawn started to rub his arm then thought better of it. Her father frowned on public displays of affection.

Jim straightened his shoulders and looked at something in the distance. "If I can, Fawn. Your mother is a worry wart. Maybe you should move into the house so she'll leave me alone. I don't like you staying out there in that cabin."

"Not a chance."

"You're teaching in town. That road is slippery in the winter and floods in the spring."

"I'll be fine." Fawn moved away toward the parking lot with one more warning. "Remember, Dad. Five o'clock. Mother will blow a gasket if you forget."

Fawn watched her father turn his back on her and stride away in the direction of the changing rooms. In moments, she would begin to fade from his thoughts as mining lead returned. He'd sunk his whole life into these lead mines dotting the surrounding hillsides. The town had literally sprung up around the jobs his mines provided. His mines and his town.

ల్లాల్ల

Garrett still couldn't believe she was standing there after all these years. His labored breathing continued until he entered the building, knowing his carefree walk could end. Fawn had been a pretty girl. Maturity turned her into a beautiful woman. Once inside, he turned to look back at Fawn who clearly appeared agitated. Under his breath he whispered, "Old man, you better stay out of my way this time."

ల్లాల్ల

Big Jim walked into where Garrett showered. His little girl was all grown up. The only thing he really knew about her was the trouble she got herself into from time to time. Maybe if he hadn't gone behind her back to discredit Garrett, things would have been different. Would he be a grandfather? He certainly would have a smart, ambitious son-in-law with the guts and courage to match his own. It was hard to admit you'd been a fool.

No. He'd done the only thing a father could do. Saving his only child from a money-chasing Horton with designs on the business was honorable. Maybe he'd been wrong about Garrett loving his only child but not about him wanting the mines. Garrett Horton ate, drank, and slept with the mines. It was in his blood. Big Jim Turnbough understood this. Hadn't he neglected his own family to get the lead out? Garrett never stopped loving the mines when Fawn married someone else. It only intensified.

એએએ

Garrett recognized the heavy footsteps of Big Jim. He knew Jim worried that he could no longer keep up with him. The miners respected him, the younger man, now. They even thought of Garrett as some kind of hero in the mines. Even though he'd graduated from the Rolla School of Mines there wasn't a job too small or too dirty Garrett wouldn't attempt.

Now it would begin all over again. Garrett knew he would go after Fawn to finish what he'd started years earlier. He'd seen the dread in the old man's frown. It didn't matter that Garrett was engaged to be married or that Fawn hated him with a passion. Fawn was trusting and fragile. Those were two of the things that he loved about her. This time, he'd have his way.

Fawn used to tell him, "What chance do I have against the charms of a country boy who possesses the looks of a god and the brains of a cunning businessman?"

The trouble was her father would still try to interfere. He was just too old to follow through this time.

"You didn't tell me Fawn was home, Jim," came a voice from one of the showers. It was Garrett.

"Teaching kindergarten this year in town. Her momma is tickled to have her home." Jim stripped off his clothes. "I'm sure you knew this."

"Grown some claws since I last saw her." Garrett couldn't help but smile as he lifted his face up into the shower. He gargled some water then sprayed it out before laughing. "Didn't seem real pleased to see me. Don't guess you know why she's so mad at me, Jim?"

"I think it's your looks," Jim offered.

Garrett stepped from the shower and wrapped a towel around his muscled body, then shook the water from his sandy-colored hair like a wet dog. "Could be." He grinned as his eyes narrowed. "You never fancied having me for a son-in-law, did you?"

"Nope," Jim answered flatly. He smiled broadly and met the eyes of the young engineer squarely. "Guess Fawn didn't either."

The smile faded from Garrett's face. Words failed him. Truth could pound the life out of you at times. Fawn didn't want him. She'd run off with some rich boy from Farmington while he was away at school. Up until today, Garrett had never seen her or even tried. There hadn't been any point. He'd heard that the marriage lasted some eighteen months before Fawn left him. She'd finished her education then moved in with Garrett's sister in Chicago.

Now she was back. The prodigal daughter. Either she was in trouble again or broke. Daddy would fix everything. He always did. Garrett pulled back his shoulders as he walked away. "I've lived this long without her, Jim. Don't see any reason to change that."

Jim turned off the shower. "Glad we see eye to eye on this, Garrett."

Garrett finished dressing then headed toward his office. He hadn't meant for the door to slam as he plopped down in his chair. Absent mindedly, Garrett began to drum a pencil on the desk as he went over the tonnage figures for the month. The numbers began to blur. Rubbing his tired eyes, he dialed a familiar number.

A soft Ozark drawl answered on the first ring. "Hello."

"Marcy Ann. Garrett." His pencil began to drum harder against the desk.

"Hi, baby. Coming home soon? Joey's got something to show you. Made it in school. First day of kindergarten. Nearly killed me."

Garrett cringed at the thought of Marcy's little boy making something for him. Unsure why he didn't want the little guy to get too attached, Garrett tried to focus on Marcy. "Can't, Marcy. Got some work to finish up here then I promised to go see Pebbles Gilliam. Got home from the hospital today. Need to talk to him."

There was a length of silence. Garrett waited. "When will you be home?"

"I don't know. I'll get a bite out, Marcy. Told the team I'd meet them to study for the mine rescue test."

"Fine."

"You're mad." Garrett sighed impatiently. Marcy was not going to be a good miner's wife. She needed to realize he could be called out in the middle of the night, working overtime without extra pay, and putting the mine first. Why didn't she understand? Fawn would've understood. A twinge of guilt surfaced. He shouldn't be comparing the two women. "I got to go, Marcy. See you later tonight. Don't wait up." The receiver clicked.

The door creaked open just as Garrett stood to leave. His best friend Shep Abney blocked his way out. "You're going to see Fawn, aren't you?"

"Damn right."

༺❀༻

Fawn, although shaken at first, recovered from seeing Garrett after she reached the cabin. It was a peaceful place. The two-room cabin was spacious enough for one person. The kitchen was quaint with cabinet doors made of glass. The locally milled counter tops came from a nearby stand of trees.

The furniture was simple—a small table and two chairs, an oak hutch that had belonged to her grandmother, a fifties model electric stove, and a refrigerator that hummed quietly.

The far end of the room boasted of two over-stuffed chairs covered in a floral print that should've been in an English manor house. They were the only new furniture Fawn bought for her little place in the woods. She placed them on each side of the fireplace. A copper tub she'd secured from a junk store in Boss held dried oak logs.

The bedroom, somewhat smaller than the kitchen, held only a brass bed covered in a patchwork quilt. A maple dresser and antique wardrobe rounded out the room. White sheers draped over the windows lifted with the slightest breeze coming from across the meadow.

Fawn walked out onto her front porch and sat down in the swing. A black kitten jumped up in her lap and began to purr as her fingers stroked his silky fur. A strange sort of peace engulfed her. It always did here.

The cabin had been a gift from her father on her tenth birthday. The memory of the night when she turned seventeen surfaced. Spring rains trapped her and Garrett alone the night of prom after they slipped off to the cabin. Before the light of day, he'd taken her virginity and enslaved her heart.

Fawn fought back tears as she stared into space. How she'd loved that scoundrel. Why couldn't he have been the knight in shining armor she'd envisioned?

"Where's that pretty head of yours?" An all too familiar voice broke her peace.

Fawn watched Garrett walk onto the porch. As he leaned against the post, a warm sensation started in her legs. He shoved his hands into the pockets of jeans that appeared to be a little too tight. She couldn't help but notice the thick hair curling at his throat where the top two buttons of his denim shirt failed to close.

Eyeing him carefully, as if he might be for hire, Fawn tossed back her hair before leveling her eyes at him. She managed to muster an icy calm, which made him straighten suddenly. "Still sneaking around like a little bad boy, I see."

His grin erased her calm as he moved toward the swing and sat down inches from her. Fawn knew if she objected, it would be a sign of weakness. He reminded her of a predator from Animal Planet that toyed with its prey before the kill. Soon he would realize she was no longer his little mouse that he could play with at his leisure.

Chapter 2

Garrett tilted his head to look at Fawn. She wasn't a kid any longer, prone to hero worship. Here stood a woman who knew what she wanted. He saw strength in Fawn's eyes. Where there had been embers of a warm-blooded woman now blazed a fiery equal. Garrett could feel his body stirring as her scent drifted up to him. The little rich girl had grown into an Ozark bobcat.

He broke the uncomfortable silence. "I'd heard you were in town, Fawn."

"I'm not surprised. Westfork is still a one-horse town that thrives on gossip." Her flat, matter-of-fact tone showed a surprising indifference toward the place of her birth.

Garrett chuckled. "So why did a big city girl like yourself come back to hell if it was so bad?"

Fawn looked at him with contempt. "I just wanted to see how the other half lived."

A hearty laugh escaped Garrett's mouth as he slipped an arm on the back of the swing behind Fawn's shoulders. "You've changed, Fawn, and for the better, I think."

"Who cares what you think?" Fawn didn't like the nearness of Garrett's hand so close to her body. She stood, dropping the kitten to the porch floor. Careful not to show that her body heat had risen several degrees, she meandered to the screen door. "I'm thirsty. Want anything?" She glanced over her shoulder at him before disappearing inside, having realized asking him such a loaded question might give him the wrong idea.

Fawn had pulled out an ice cube tray from the dated refrigerator when she heard the screen door squeak open then snap close. "I don't remember asking you to come in, Garrett Horton." It was an effort to force her voice to be icy, considering how hard her heart pounded against her breast. She filled two glasses with the ice then poured some sweet tea from the pitcher sitting on the counter.

She handed Garrett a glass as she lifted her own to touch her face. Her eyes closed. She loved the way the cold smacked the heat away. When she opened them, Fawn found Garrett's blue eyes looking over the top of his glass.

It was difficult not to focus on his mouth, especially

when he lowered the glass and smiled. Moisture clung to his lips like a sweet invitation.

Fawn took a deep breath and leaned against the counter before forcing a quick gulp.

"Remember when we were kids, Jeanie Fawn?" He looked around the room as if seeing it for the first time. "I'd slip off from home and come out here to check on you and my sister."

A smile forced its way onto Fawn's lips. "Yes. Sometimes we'd even let you eat the cookies we made for being our knight in shining armor."

"You promised your momma you wouldn't use the stove." He laughed. "I never told." He moved toward the bedroom and filled up the doorway with his hard body. "I loved this place." His coarse voice almost sounded melancholy.

Fawn didn't like where this was headed. Garrett standing in the bedroom had gotten her into more trouble than she wished to repeat. She jiggled her glass to make the ice cubes tinkle, drawing his eyes back to her. The unexpected pain in his blue eyes made her stomach lurch. But it disappeared so quickly Fawn wondered if the look was a figment of her imagination.

Garrett turned back toward her. "Can I have a refill?"

"No. I think you should go."

Garrett ignored her and poured himself another glass. "Nobody makes sweet tea like your momma but I swear, Jeanie Fawn, yours is damn close."

This time he drank the glass in several gulps.

"Don't call me Jeanie Fawn."

Garrett sat the glass down a little too hard on the counter, making Fawn cringe. "Sorry. Old habits die hard, Fawn." He dragged her name out like it was taffy. "How's the job? Marcy Ann tells me you're Joey's teacher." Garrett needed to keep his body in check and mentioning his fiancée might help.

"Does your sister approve of your current living arrangements?" Fawn remembered how Marcy had tormented Garrett's sister in high school. That had been a long time ago. People change.

"She knows. Says I should give it up and marry you." His comment caused Fawn to choke on her drink.

"Your sister is very amusing."

"She sends her love by the way. Saw her a few weeks ago in Oklahoma."

"Pity you didn't stay." Fawn made an effort to sound flippant. "Now if you don't mind, Garrett, I'm really busy." Her eyes glanced at the door.

Garrett poured his ice cubes in the sink, noting that Fawn had straightened as if she'd walk him to the door. "If that's what you want."

Fawn rolled her eyes up to the ceiling in frustration. "Of course, it's what I want."

Before she could step away, Garrett pulled her into his arms. The familiar feeling of strength and being safe washed over her. She knew he was waiting for her to squirm then surrender to his charms like she used to do in the old days. She'd pretend to object and he'd laugh until she bombarded him with her kisses. A wall of composure engulfed her this time as her eyes met his with a narrowed determination.

"Well?" Taking a deep breath seemed to help. "I see you still think you are all that to the females around here. Sorry to disappoint you, but I'm not a member of the Garrett Horton fan club."

Garrett smiled through gritted teeth. "You don't fool me, Fawn. I can feel your heart hammering in that pretty little body of yours. Nothing has changed between us. You still need me and I still want you."

"You're crazy." She placed her hands against his chest and pushed while she still had the resolve to do so.

"I don't know why you've come home, but if you think we can put the past behind us, you're the one who is crazy. You owe me an explanation for running out on me."

"I owe you!" She managed to free herself of his arms only to be grabbed around the wrist. "I didn't realize how much I loathed you until this very minute."

Garrett jerked on her wrist so that she fell back into his arms. "The feeling is mutual, Fawn. Why did you leave me? Did your father make you?" Garrett demanded, tightening his embrace.

"Get out of my house, Garrett Horton, or so help me I'll have you fired from Turnbough Lead."

Garrett laughed. "Fired? Go ahead. Try. If there's one thing your old man loves more than you, it's the company. He knows I'm the future for Turnbough Lead. I'm the fair-haired boy, sweetheart. Don't threaten me and don't tease me." He released her so quickly that she fell back against the counter.

She rubbed her wrists. "Stay away from me, Garrett."

"With pleasure, Fawn. I wanted to see for myself if you really were still that spoiled little rich girl everyone claims."

"Now you know." She tried to hide the pain of hearing his words by dropping her eyes to the floor. The slam of the screen door triggered a flood of tears down her expensive makeup.

The hate that threatened to well up inside her evaporated at remembering Garrett's arms holding her against his chest. She'd forgotten the strength he possessed. Garrett was a dangerous combination of power, good looks, and brains. His sharp blue eyes reminded her how she'd once wanted their children to look. With a disgusted sigh, Fawn wiped her eyes and promised herself she'd make a conscious effort to put the sensations of Garrett Horton out of her life-again.

༺༻

Fawn hid away in the cabin or took long walks

through the woods all weekend. She didn't even attend church with her parents at the local Baptist church, afraid she might run into Garrett along the way. Solitude and reflection went a long way at mending the wall against the charms of her former lover, which she'd spent ten years building.

She'd been shaken to the core after Garrett had pulled her into his arms. All the years of buried passion rushed forth inside her to the point she thought she might burst into flame before his very eyes. But her hatefulness had vanquished the knight she once adored. If only he hadn't betrayed her.

At one point in the weekend, Fawn got the courage to drag out the pictures her father had given her so many years earlier. The reason she'd kept them remained a mystery. Maybe it was because she needed a constant reminder that Garrett was a lying dog who only wanted her to get his hands on Turnbough Lead.

The pictures were proof he'd cheated on her two weeks before their wedding while he was away at school. There were pictures of him entering a strip club in St. Roberts and necking with some floosy in his old pickup truck in front of a cheap motel in Rolla. Those and the drunken party during Greek Week at his fraternity were the tame shots. The photo of a girl sitting half naked in his lap then a second one of her in bed with Garrett had been the painful beginning of the end.

Knowing how Garrett liked to plan for their future,

Fawn up and left. Not even a note. That would take him by surprise. She left a message on her father's voice mail at work and let him take care of the inevitable end of the relationship. Fawn thought Garrett would explode with anger at her leaving. But he didn't. He never even tried to find her to ask why. In some ways, that hurt the worst. It was one more piece of evidence that he cared nothing for her.

Garrett had planned to take a couple of semesters off to have enough money to continue at the Rolla School of Mines since he would now have a wife. Fawn planned to continue getting her teaching degree on the satellite campus of Southwest Baptist University in Salem. He said he wanted her to be able to take care of herself if anything ever happened to him working in the mines. They would both laugh, knowing Fawn would never have to work another day if she chose.

But Garrett never quit school. Fawn often wondered how far in debt he went to finish school so quickly. He was a poor country boy with big ideas and no money.

She remembered how his sister had kept her informed of Garrett's graduation and tried to convince her to return home. Even though Garrett's sister didn't understand the sudden breakup, she never turned her back on Fawn.

Just when Fawn started to feel better about her decision to move back to Westfork, Garrett showed up on her doorstep. That must never happen again. She wanted no part of his life and he couldn't take any more of hers.

The weekend gave her the courage to go back into the world on Monday morning to her teaching job. Marcy Ann, the current love interest of Garrett, was waiting for her at the classroom door. A dread floated up Fawn's spin like a chill. Marcy's little boy was one of her kindergarteners.

Marcy Ann and Fawn had never been friends in high school. They faced off like opponents in most school activities. The envy Marcy carried in her little group of popular girls usually directed cruel taunts at Garrett's sister and, of course, Fawn. The two friends suffered jokes and pranks more times than she wished to remember. Fawn never fought back.

Now here the foe stood with a sheepish look of uncertainty. Fawn wondered if the woman remembered all the misery she'd put her through as a teenager. Did she also remember how Garrett always came to the rescue when he caught wind of anyone bothering his sister and best friend? Part of her hoped so.

"Hello, Marcy." Fawn unlocked her door, trying to balance a briefcase and a to-go cup of coffee from Cat's General Store.

"Here let me help." Marcy took the cup carefully as if it contained the secret of life.

Fawn swung the door open. "Thanks. It's good to see you. We didn't really get to talk much on Meet the Parents night. Where's Joey?"

"He has a slight temperature. Can I take some work home for him? He's so afraid he'll get behind." Marcy's voice sounded nervous. "He really likes you, Fawn."

Fawn picked up some papers off her desk. "The feeling is mutual. He's a smart child. He is going to do just fine in school, Marcy." Fawn remembered that Marcy almost didn't graduate. "You're lucky to have such a terrific little guy." Offering a friendly smile, Fawn handed her the papers. "Tell him I will miss him so much today." She really did love the little guy.

Looking down at the papers, Marcy smiled with pride. "Thank you, Fawn. All the mothers say their kids are just crazy about you."

Fawn chuckled. Marcy was about to make a point. "Well, a boy's first crush is usually his kindergarten teacher. So I'm a lucky girl."

"Guess that doesn't surprise you none. You were always popular with the boys."

Fawn had an over powering urge to correct Marcy's grammar but thought better of it. "The only boy who ever dared take me out was Garrett Horton and you know it, Marcy." She tried to lighten the mood with a soft laugh. "Garrett's sister was the one who needed bodyguards to keep the throngs away. I was the ugly-duckling sidekick."

"Have you seen Garrett since you come back?"

And there it was. A checkup.

Fawn could feel her smile turn to plastic. She, of all people, knew how difficult it was being in love with a man who might not love you back. "I saw him the other day at the mine when I went to see my father. They were coming out from underground together. I understand congratulations are in order. When are you getting married?"

The tenseness in Marcy's shoulders lessened. "Donno. Garrett has a lot of work to do with the mine rescue team. Probably not before next June." Marcy shoved the papers into her oversized purse and turned to go. She stopped at the door and turned back to face Fawn. "I'd do anything for Garrett. My Joey and I love him more than life itself, Fawn."

Fawn felt herself sag with some unknown grief. The mere touch of Garrett's hand on Friday had sent her pulse racing for two days, and for what? Marcy was in a life-or-death struggle over a man who would never love her as much as a piece of hard rock he dug out of the ground.

Sucking up what little mental resolve she had left, Fawn nodded an acknowledgement. "From what I hear, Garrett is a new man since you've come into his life. I'm very happy for you, Marcy. Really."

For the first time Marcy smiled radiantly. "Thank you, Fawn. For everything."

No hidden meaning there, thought Fawn, feeling a sense of loss all over again. Sucking in all the air her lungs could hold, Fawn composed herself for the hundredth time since Garrett had surprised her at the cabin. If there was one person worse off than herself, it was Marcy

Ann Davies. The poor girl was so in love with Garrett that she'd probably stoop to anything to keep him. It was a point worth remembering. Marcy Ann, once a mean spirited girl in high school, could threaten any hopes of a second chance at happiness. If she thought Garrett was sniffing around Fawn like a hungry hound dog again, Marcy Ann might make trouble.

Chapter 3

Garrett still nursed a bruised ego after leaving Fawn a few days earlier. She'd affected him more than he realized. The reoccurring thought of how she'd abandoned him just weeks before their wedding, with only a snide voice mail her father took great pleasure in playing for him, still burned in his gut.

Big Jim never said Fawn had gotten cold feet, but only implied it. When pressed a little harder, Jim admitted there might be someone else but he wasn't sure. Garrett knew that had to be a lie. Anything that had to do with the Turnboughs was going to get back to the big guy in charge. Fawn had jilted Garrett in the worse possible way. Not only did she call off the wedding, but she did so because of a fling she'd had with some playboy in Farmington. How could he have been so wrong about someone he'd known most of his life?

The only nice thing Big Jim had ever done for Garrett was give him an interest-free loan to finish school and a position at Turnbough Lead when he finished. It was the least he could do, or so he said. Garrett was grateful. Westfork was his home and he loved it. Being able to stay there with a good paying job was more than a poor boy like him could ever hope for. At least he wouldn't have to slave in the timber at a local logging company like his father had.

"Where's your head, buddy?" It was Shep Gilliam, his best friend.

Garrett frowned and put on his hard hat. "Let's get the lead out, Shep." He moved toward the door when Shep raised an arm to stop him.

"How'd it go with Fawn?"

"It was a mistake." Garrett pushed through and made his way to the head frame where an open cage elevator waited to take him down nearly a thousand feet into the lead mines. Shep was at his side, humming some country song. Garrett was glad not to be pressed for more information.

The cage bounced to a stop, just like always, and Garrett opened the wire door into his world—damp, dirty, and looking like a cavernous place where dinosaurs could easily walk. The smell of diesel reached his nose. He greeted several men good heartedly and started his day with renewed purpose, in hopes the sensation of holding the love of his life in his arms again would fade.

During lunch, Big Jim came down into the mine as he always did, to visit with the men and then spend the afternoon going over the work his people completed in the last twenty-four hours. He was slow to encourage them, so Garrett tried to over compensate for the old man's lack of praise. Sometimes, it was a nod of approval or a slap on the back, but it meant high praise coming from the mine captain.

Garrett rushed to jump on the cage with Big Jim that day at four. "Jim, we need to talk."

The old man frowned and stepped back for Garrett to squeeze in next to three others who planned to ride up. The men were tired, dirty, and hungry. No words passed between them as the cage lifted swiftly to above ground. The clank of the accordion wire door as it opened made the men step with purpose out into the late afternoon sun. Squinting at its beauty and inhaling the fresh Ozark air, the men, along with Garrett, thanked God another day had passed without an accident.

"What is it, Garrett? Make it fast. I told Momma I'd take her to Salem to that new fish restaurant. Don't know why we have to go all that way for fish. The Westfork Inn has the best catfish in Iron County. Women." Big Jim walked at a brisk pace. Age had not taken his power to make a physical impression.

"Slow down, will ya?" Garrett had worked hard and

didn't really want a confrontation in front of the men.

They entered the building where the showers washed the lead dust from weary miners wanting to head home to their families and girlfriends.

Garrett waited until he'd taken his shower to make his way to Big Jim's office in the main building. The old man took a quick shower then hurried off without saying another word to his mine captain. Garrett knew the routine—walk away and pretend you have more pressing matters. Big Jim practiced the strategy when he didn't want to change procedure or correct a mistake. Finding out you weren't omniscient from a Horton was hard for the old man to swallow. Garrett would fight for what he knew to be right until Big Jim caved. The dance of power between them grew more familiar with each passing day. The fight had to occur to save face, or maybe it was Jim's ego on the line. Garrett didn't really know or care, but he wasn't going to be putting his men in danger for bigger tonnage and more money.

"Jim, got a minute?" He walked in on his boss without knocking.

This always irritated Jim so Garrett made sure he always did it. The dance between them was as familiar as the lead dust that washed into the tailings pond on the other side of the mine. When Jim continued shuffling papers without speaking, Garrett pulled out a chair and flopped down, and waited.

"What is it, Garrett? Your men being a bunch of crybabies again?"

"No."

Big Jim stopped and leaned back in his chair. "Not still talking about forming a union, I hope."

"The last raise you gave them stopped that. They didn't even mind that the medical insurance stayed the same. What I came to talk to you about—"

The phone rang and Jim snatched it up. He held up his hand to stop Garrett. Another power play. The conversation was pretty one sided so Garrett guessed it was Jim's wife.

"Hurry up, Garrett. I gotta pick up Momma."

The frown meant to intimidate only made Garrett smile. "Whose idea was it to start mining the pillars in south end of the mine?"

"Charleston."

"That new superintendent you hired has his head up his ass."

"I suppose I should have hired you. Is that what this is about? You're licking your bruised ego because I passed over you? Again."

Garrett could feel his face turning red as he clenched his fists. "You hired a desk jockey from St. Louis who has a degree in geology, not mining."

"He's worked all over the country, Garrett, and you know it."

"That, in itself, is a little suspicious, don't you think? Why would all those other mining companies let him go if he was such a catch? Peabody Coal certainly didn't stop him when he got out of St. Louis. He's full of textbook crap and no real underground experience."

"So you say. Charleston says lead prices aren't going to go any higher for another three years. There might be a glut on the market after that and prices will fall. I want to get the biggest bang for my buck. Those pillars are the highest grade lead found anywhere in the world. We'll get top dollar for that."

"And you'll risk bringing the mine down on our heads."

"There's a way to avoid that, Mr. College Man." Big Jim never finished college but no one knew more about mining than him. "I got a bigger payroll now thanks to you."

"So this is my fault?" Garrett snapped. "Let me set up a plan to mine those pillars in a slow, select way. We don't need to take many to make a profit, Jim."

"I'll see what Charleston thinks."

"Don't tell him it was me or he'll refuse to listen. You're smarter than this, Jim." Garrett stood up and moved to the door.

Big Jim narrowed his eyes as his hand rubbed the stubble on his chin. "Get the hell out of my office. And knock next time." he yelled as Garrett meandered out, his deep laugh echoing down the hall.

September turned to October before Fawn had the opportunity to see Garrett again. She worked hard at staying out of town and out of sight. Minding her own business seemed to be the best way to avoid contact with him. He had never reappeared at the cabin and Fawn felt a little regret, knowing she wished he had returned.

Time forced her to realize she could apologize for the poor behavior. Why she'd acted so cool and aloof had been a mere defense mechanism, afraid Garrett would take advantage of her. Apparently, Fawn had been mistaken about any torch he carried for her. He was no more interested in her than she was in him. Comfortable in her new found freedom, she ventured out into Westfork on the weekend of Old Miner's Day.

People from as far away as Rolla came to take free mine tours, sample funnel cakes, and snatch up Ozark crafts made by local artists. Musical groups performed throughout the weekend. A parade with the new Miss Old Miner's Day started the Saturday celebration off. Everyone liked to brag, "If it was Old Miner's Day, the weather would be perfect."

Games for the children had already begun on the parking lot of the small strip mall next to the bank. Since streets had been blocked off, people strolled as they munched on candied apples or corn on the cob.

Every storefront had decorated for the occasion—

colorful mums, gourds, pumpkins, dried cornstalks, and flowers. It made strolling in and out of shops a kind of eye candy for the tourists. Trees blazed with autumn color as fallen leaves crunched beneath the feet of little boys stomping to stir up the dust.

A blue-grass band had center stage. Fawn stopped to listen and clapped after each number. She'd forgotten how much she loved the music of the Ozarks. A warm feeling began to spread throughout her body, knowing she'd made the right decision in moving back to Westfork.

Mixed with the smell of fried fish at the Boy Scout booth and the roasted pork sandwiches of the Baptist church, Fawn caught a whiff of wood smoke from chimneys in town. Earlier in the day, the temperature hovered around forty degrees. But the afternoon sun mixed with a light breeze made the autumn heat feel like a warm cup of tea. Her eyes surveyed the small groups of people gathered to gossip, the displays of mining information under the awnings of the Dollar General Store, and the throngs of runners waiting in front of the grocery store to begin their Hard Rock Run.

Proud to be home, she glanced at the large sign in front of the grandstand. "If it can't be grown, it has to be mined."

Fawn met up with her parents and continued through the crowd, stopping to speak to old friends. Her heart grew light and carefree as the warm October sun beat down on her head. She hooked her arm through her mother's and felt an occasional squeeze of affection.

Her mother beamed. "I'm so glad you're home with us again, Fawn."

Nell Turnbough's gentle voice matched her smooth, wrinkle-free face. Only her silver hair hinted at age. Although a head shorter than Fawn, Nell carried herself like a queen. Everywhere she went, people spoke to her with respect and love befitting the wife of Jim Turnbough. No words of gossip would pass their lips as long as Fawn was at her mother's side.

"Look, Fawn," her mother exclaimed seeing the Hortons stroll in their direction "Sarah," Nell called to Garrett's mother, waving all the while. "Sarah, over here."

Fawn sighed in anxiousness. "Mother."

"Oh, pooh. Sarah holds no ill will against you," Nell insisted.

As she approached, Sarah's eyes were wary as she glanced at Fawn. Immediately, she hugged Nell then turned to Fawn. "Hello, Jeanie Fawn." Her sweet smile turned timid and unsure.

"Mrs. Horton."

"Since when am I Mrs. Horton?" She continued to smile.

Fawn didn't know how it happened but suddenly she reached for Sarah with outstretched arms and found herself holding the tall woman close to her breasts. Fawn sniffed back the tears she feared would escape.

"Oh, Sarah. It's so good to see you."

Memories of times she'd spent at Sarah's table, eating supper and sleeping over with her best friend Kathleena, reminded her the Hortons were the brothers and sisters Fawn had never received from her own parents.

Sarah gave Fawn a little shake. "Why haven't you come to see me? I'm terribly hurt. Don't you like me no more?"

The thought of facing Garrett's mother after what she'd done to her son was not a scene Fawn wanted to experience. But here Sarah stood before her now, the love still in those round eyes.

Fawn laughed as she became aware of an approaching figure out of the corner of her eye. "I adore you and I'll drop by this week. Have you heard from Kathleena?"

"She'll be home Christmas. I expect you for Christmas dinner just like always, young lady."

"O—oh, Sarah," Fawn stammered. "I don't know."

"Of course, you'll come." Garrett's self-assured voice sounded more masculine than she remembered. A hot spear of recognition shot through her body as Garrett came to stand beside her. "It wouldn't be Christmas without you, Fawn. You're one of the family." Garrett slipped an arm around Nell. "Hi, gorgeous. When are you going to run away with me? I still say you got all the looks in the family."

Nell giggled like a school girl and patted Garrett's hard midriff with affection. "Oh, Garrett, hush."

Garrett placed a quick kiss on Nell's cheek then his mother's. His satisfaction in knowing Nell had always approved of him made his boldness justified. "Now if you'll excuse me, ladies, the square dance is about to begin and I'm taking Fawn away from you."

Before Fawn could protest, Garrett maneuvered her onto his arm and dragged her toward the gathering dancers.

"No, Garrett, please."

Fawn decided her protest was a little too flimsy. Couldn't she just shake him off and escape? That probably would only cause a bigger scene. Eyebrows were already beginning to arch as Garrett swung her in front of him and began to bow like a gentleman.

"Relax." He looked like a devil in blue jeans with his lopsided grin and piercing blue eyes. The sun glinted off his sandy blond hair. "What can happen? You're surrounded by hundreds of people."

As the fiddle began its lyrical tune and the caller instructed the dancers, Fawn let herself be swung around the circle in a grand right and left until she once again met up with Garrett. He turned her around with extra gusto. Fawn felt her hands tighten on Garrett's arm, making his blue eyes swallow her whole. They might be surrounded by hundreds of people, but there was no mistaking where Garrett's thoughts were headed.

The sensation of being captured overwhelmed Fawn. She knew her body was powerless to resist as the dance continued, then another and still another until she grew breathless. Reluctantly, she pushed Garrett away, letting a giddy laugh escape her mouth.

Feeling the heightened color in her face, Fawn touched her cheeks and smiled. "No more, Garrett. I've had enough."

Garrett smiled as one eyebrow lifted. "I don't think I'll ever say that about you, Fawn."

As Fawn frowned, Garrett nodded. "See you 'round, Fawn."

Like a phantom, he disappeared into the throng of people who closed in around him.

Fawn stood alone. When she turned to leave, she saw Marcy Ann glaring. A feeling of guilt washed over her. Fawn lifted her head and tried to leave with some semblance of grace to find her mother.

Nell sat at a picnic table nursing a cola. She watched the gaiety of the miners and their families. "They love this day." Nell smiled up at her daughter, tears shining in her eyes. "I hope your father can live to see…"

"Daddy will live to be a hundred, Mother. You say that every year. By the way, what did Dr. Tony have to say about him? You never told me."

"The usual." Nell waved with a hanky she'd pulled from her leather bag. "I had hoped that you would be settled by now so someone else could run the mines. Your father and I could spend our remaining years traveling and enjoying the grandchildren."

Fawn put her face in her hands with exasperation. "I knew I should have never gone with Garrett to dance."

"You look so right for each other, honey."

"He's a barracuda."

"Sarah loves you like a daughter."

Fawn couldn't resist a snarl. Her own mother was Garrett's captive. "And you love all that phony baloney Garrett dishes out. Perhaps a gift of a shovel will be appropriate at Christmas, considering all the you-know-what he spreads."

"He still loves you, Fawn."

Fawn turned to leave. "I'm going back to the house. Would you like for me to take you to Daddy before I go?"

"No." Nell's voice was soft and faraway. "I'll be fine, Fawn. You run along."

Fawn turned but couldn't resist getting in the last word. "I loathe Garrett, Mother, so don't get your heart set on us getting back together."

Nell looked up at her beautiful child and smiled. "Mothers know about these things, Fawn. You have Garrett under your skin. Just deal with it this time. I'm getting old and very impatient." Her eyes turned back to the crowd, and she didn't say another word.

Chapter 4

Fawn bristled at her mother's words. She stormed off at a rapid pace to find her black Porsche at the edge of town. Once there, she quickly sped down the highway toward the Turnbough home. Her speedometer reached seventy as she zipped past a policeman hiding on a side road. Fawn knew he wouldn't dare follow. No one would. She was big Jim Turnbough's daughter. Heaven help the man who ever gave his little girl a ticket.

Eighty miles per hour.

Why was she punishing herself? It was Garrett who was wreaking havoc on her senses.

Fifty miles per hour.

Forty miles per hour.

She wasn't going to die because of him.

Loose gravel flew up to crack the windshield as she whipped onto the black top driveway of what was known as Pucky Huddle Hill. Big Jim built his mansion there for everyone to see from a distance. The road was a private one, all two miles of it. Fawn loved the way her Porsche hugged each curve as her foot grew heavy again.

The image of Garrett rolling across satin sheets to capture her in the dark of night was much like driving the devilish black car. As the speedometer climbed once more, her pulse raced. The memory of how Garrett slid his large rough hands around her waist earlier was almost more than she could handle. He'd twirled her until she'd lost her balance, only to fall against him. Garrett had politely helped her regain her composure, never changing his outward expression of satisfaction. No one but Fawn saw the look of victory in those blue eyes that still managed to ignite a fire deep inside her.

They were two souls destined to tangle in the bonds of love one more time. It would not only be a battle of wills but of desires. This time all mercy would be cast to the wind—no prisoners taken for further humiliation and heartbreak.

Fawn smiled as she screeched to a halt in the circle drive in front of her father's home.

Maybe knowing what would inevitably happen between them would steel her heart against the danger it posed. "You're going to be sorry I ever came back, Garrett Horton."

The soft hum of a Lexus pulled to a stop in front of Fawn's small cabin. It was late. Music continued to play on satellite radio as Stanley Fulbright pushed a button to lower the windows. Fawn could tell he was very pleased with himself sitting there in the five hundred dollar suit he'd purchased in St. Louis. He made a point earlier to tell her the cost, as if that might impress her.

It didn't.

Stanley was handsome enough—a little too polished for Fawn's taste, but others considered him quite sophisticated. She reasoned it was because he was a lawyer. That didn't impress her either. His hands were soft. Everyone knew he hired others to do anything too strenuous. Fawn wondered if he'd ever mowed the grass or taken out his own garbage.

She had her father to thank for that kind of upbringing. It didn't matter that they were the richest people in three counties. She'd learned to help her mother clean the house, keep a vegetable garden, and do the dishes every night. A dishwasher couldn't replace all those chats she and her mother had after the evening meal. Only on Sundays and holidays did the dishes get shoved into the dishwasher.

At the time, Fawn had complained. Now she was grateful her parents had given her a work ethic. Everyone thought of her as a rich girl who had everything. If they only knew the truth, they'd probably roll on the ground laughing at the irony.

Fawn found herself barely listening to Stanley, who was rambling on about the country club. A smile and nod seemed to give him encouragement to continue the mindless, self-absorbed chatter he had perfected.

"You know, Fawn, this is our third date in two weeks."

Fawn looked surprised. "Really? Hmm." That was about all she could manage to say.

"I can't believe my luck." He reached for her hand as she quickly opened the car door and slid out. It only took a second for him to join her on the other side of the car.

Fawn paused listening to autumn crickets sing their song. The smell of dew on freshly mowed grass reminded her of an earthy perfume. As she started up the porch steps, Stanley cut her off.

"You and Garrett's sister were always the prettiest girls in Iron County." He laid his hand on hers, which she slowly slipped away. "I never could understand what you saw in that hick, Garrett Horton." And there it was. Jealousy of something Stanley would never understand. "He was such a jerk," Stanley said and laughed at his own words.

Fawn eyed Stanley as she fought the urge to sock him in the nose. "The Hortons are good people. Hard working and dedicated to family. I loved that about them. They treated me well."

Stanley laughed again followed by a snide retort. "They were just after your money. Everyone knew that."

Fawn burned with a protective instinct. "Is that why you've started coming around, Stanley? You think I have money? Because if it is, you need to know that my father has left me nothing in his will," she lied. "He believes I need to make my own way in the world. That's why I got a teaching degree."

Stanley snorted. "Like I believe he wouldn't take care of his only child." This time Stanley reached out and stroked Fawn's arm. "I just want a chance with the most beautiful woman I've ever known." It sounded a little too smooth and a little too rehearsed.

Well aware of a string of one night stands Stanley bragged about to his golf buddies in Farmington, Fawn could only muster an accusing chuckle. "Oh, Stanley, do you really think I'm going to fall for that line? I know all about your little girl friends in the old lead belt."

Sticking out his lip as if wounded, Stanley dared put his other hand of her waist. "Not true. I would give my right arm to be with you, Fawn. I was half crazy watching you all evening at the club. You've grown into quite a beauty. You were a pretty girl but now…" Stanley took a step closer and pulled her into his arms.

Fawn pushed him back and continued up the steps. "I'm sorry, Stanley. I hope I haven't given you the wrong impression of where this was going. I thought it might be nice to have dinner and talk about the old days. I'm really not looking for a *boyfriend*." The last word out of her mouth sounded like an insult. "I'm going in, Stanley. It's been a long day. Thanks for dinner."

Stanley had followed her to the screen door. "How about a drink?"

Fawn paused at the door. "Not tonight, Stanley."

Before she knew what was happening, Stanley jerked her into his arms, burying his mouth against hers. He forced her lips open as she squirmed to be released from his hard tongue. Like a glass of ice water being poured down her back, Fawn shivered with revulsion at Stanley's rough penetration of her mouth. She jumped away and wiped the back of her hand across her lips. "Stop it, Stanley. Go home!"

Stanley took a step forward as his voice changed into a warning. "Isn't that what you wanted?"

"No. Why would you think such a thing?"

"I just thought you were sending me signals you wanted me to come in for a little more than a night cap." He came so close that Fawn retreated back to the steps. "You're just like Garrett's sister, a tease."

Fawn halted. "Leave Kathleena out of this." She could feel her knees turn to jelly as she realized how alone and far from town she lived. Why hadn't she remembered how Stanley was a cheater and liar in high school? He'd beaten Kathleena out of being valedictorian by stealing the answers to a biology exam which put him over the top.

Stanley pinned her against the porch railing. "I love how you smell. You've turned into quite a prize. You were such a skinny thing in high school. Now you've filled out in all the right places." He ran his hand down her back. When he touched her bottom, Fawn twisted free. As she clumsily started down the steps, she tripped, falling to the ground. Laughing, Stanley stalked her then lunged to grab her. She managed to roll away just as he hit the ground with a thud. Scrambling to her feet, she tried to run past him onto the porch, hoping to make it inside to safety. But Stanley caught her by the ankle as she jumped up, causing her to fall on the steps.

"You always did think you were better than the rest of us," he snapped as his fingers dug into her ankle.

"Evenin'," came a deep, familiar voice from the far end of the house.

Stanley jerked his hand back to his side. "Who's there?"

A flashlight beam swung back and forth in small circles as a man approached. He flashed the light up into his face for only an instant. "Just me."

"Garrett Horton. I should have known." Stanley snorted. "Out coon hunting no doubt."

Garrett smiled wolfishly as he stepped closer for Stanley. He wanted him to look into his cold blue eyes. His head cocked toward Fawn who had backed up the steps of her porch. He aimed the light at her clothes before turning his head back toward Stanley. "Take a spill,

Jeanie Fawn?" Before she could answer, Garrett smiled at Stanley. "Remember how clumsy this girl was in school?"

A nervous Stanley loosened his tie with one finger. "Yeah. I remember."

"Had to watch her like a hawk."

Stanley cleared his throat. "Guess she hasn't changed."

"Neither have I, Stanley." Garrett thumped him good naturedly on the back. He pointed his light at Stanley's car. "Import?"

"Of course." Stanley dared to sound indignant as he rushed to the driver's side. He felt Garrett's breath on the back of his neck as he tried to open the door. Just when he thought he might escape, Garrett rammed the flashlight in the small of his back. Stanley fell forward and hit his chin on the edge of the door.

Garrett fell against him with his full weight. "You listen to me, you worthless sack of horse manure." His voice had taken on the growl of a pit bull. "If you ever come around Fawn again, you damn well better keep your pants on." Garrett sighed and shook his head. "Just stay away from her. You understand that, Mr. Harvard Law School?" No response. Garrett rammed the light harder into his back. "Do you?"

"Yes! Now let me go."

Garrett stepped back and patted Stanley on the shoulder. "Good to see you, Stan. Let's have a beer sometime and talk about the good ole days." Garrett laughed good naturedly as Stanley jumped into his car and locked the door.

"When hell freezes over."

"Until then, good buddy." Garrett waved as Stanley flipped him off then spun his car around. In seconds, he was gone.

Garrett looked up at the shadow of Fawn standing on the stairs. His cowboy boots sounded loud as they hit the bottom step. When he moved closer, he saw that Fawn was paralyzed with terror at what had nearly happened. Seeing those eyes full of pain made him reassess letting Stanley escape.

"Guess ole Stanley is probably the stupidest lawyer in the state of Missouri." Garrett grinned as he stepped a little closer. "I think I scared your boyfriend off, Fawn. I doubt he'll be coming back any time soon. You know me. Never could mind my own business when it came to you girls." A mischievous tone made him look boyish in the moonlight.

Fawn choked on her tears as she ran down the steps into Garrett's arms. She heard the flashlight drop as she buried her face into a familiar shoulder. In one swoop, he'd lifted her up and carried her inside. She clung to him as if he were a life line.

Setting her feet down, Garrett flipped on the kitchen light. He pushed the brown hair that stuck to a tear-streaked face behind her ears. "Are you all right?" She nodded and sniffed. Then she was crying and clinging to him again. "You want me to take you to your mom's?"

She shook her head. So he held her tightly until the tears stopped. The press of her body against his was unnerving. Every part of him wanted to pick her up again and carry her to the bedroom. But that would be a mistake. One night's gratitude could turn out to be a disaster.

He stroked her hair and rubbed the middle of her back like any good friend would do. Could she tell that his body had stirred to life? Did she just think he'd come to the rescue one more time?

As he embraced her, his thoughts turned back to another time he'd saved her from certain harm. It was a time when Fawn wanted to rebel against her father. She'd taken a notion to ride one of her father's Arabian horses which wasn't quite saddle broken.

"Stay off that horse, Jeanie Fawn," Garrett warned. "I'll saddle you that Morgan over there. She's small and gentle as a lamb. Besides, you've never ridden bareback. You'll break your fool neck. Now get away from there."

Garrett had turned only for a minute to get the Morgan horse. But Fawn got on the Arabian without another thought. The half-wild horse ran away with her, Fawn screaming at the top of her lungs.

He'd taken the Morgan without saddling her first and took out after Fawn. He'd found her nearly unconscious and with a broken leg. Garrett had carried her home, then stole her father's truck before driving her to the hospital.

He took the blame for her fall. When he told Big Jim he didn't realize the horse was half crazy or he would never have put her on his back, he got a tongue lashing he cringed at even today. He stayed all night in the hospital with Fawn, sleeping on the floor next to the bed.

"I'll never tell Big Jim," he promised the next morning before she went into surgery.

"Garrett," she whispered now. Her fingers ran through his thick hair.

Feeling himself lose control, Garrett did not want to take up where Stanley had left off. That wasn't going to happen with Fawn. She was experiencing gratefulness, not love. Memories stirred up the past, not what could be the future. Garrett didn't want that. When he took Fawn, it would be because she couldn't live without him any longer.

He stepped back and hunched down to look into her eyes. "Better?"

She nodded almost shyly, trying to hide smeared eye makeup. "I must look a fright," she sniffed.

He pulled her to one of the over-stuffed chairs and guided her to sit. "Come on. I'll make you a cup of tea just like your momma does it."

Fawn now offered a smile. "You? Make a cup of tea?"

"I watched Nell do this a zillion times when we were growing up." He started looking for a cup and proceeded to heat the kettle of water. "How hard could it be?"

"So handy. I had no idea."

"Don't let it get out. Marcy Ann will have me doing dishes." He laughed then sobered as their eyes clashed. He'd forgotten all about Marcy Ann until the very second her name slipped from his lips. By the look on Fawn's face, so had she. She diverted her eyes to the floor.

While the kettle heated on the stove, Fawn excused herself to clean up in the bathroom. When she returned, Garrett had managed to get a fire roaring in the stone fireplace. Its warmth filled the kitchen.

"Hmm. I think I'll sleep in the chair tonight next to the fire." Fawn dragged a brush through her tangled hair. She realized Garrett watched each stroke as if he were doing it himself. With the start of the whistling kettle, he finished making her tea.

He bowed, bearing a faded metal tray with two cups of steaming tea. "As promised."

"Thank you." She took the mug with one hand while laying the brush down on the old cupboard. Garrett had grown quiet. Did he feel guilt being with her instead of Marcy? "You don't have to stay, Garrett. I'm fine now. Really."

He watched her take one of the chairs by the fire and he tried to sit down opposite her without spilling his drink. "Still trying to get rid of me?" He took a sip of his tea and frowned. "You really should learn to make coffee, Fawn. A man can't survive on this."

Fawn smiled, in spite of feeling on guard. "My ex-husband said I made lousy coffee."

"No wonder it didn't last." Garrett sounded flippant as he smirked.

Fawn couldn't help but chuckle as her eyes met his. They were liquid fire. "What did you say to Stanley?"

"I think the jest of the conversation was if he ever pulled another stupid stunt like he did tonight, he'd be singing soprano in the Baptist choir." His calm voice did not match the turbulence in his gut.

"And why were you even here in the first place?"

"Like the man said, I was coon hunting. Lost my dogs."

"Oh, please," Fawn moaned. "You can do better than that." She hoped as much anyway.

Garrett sat his cup down and stood. He stared bitterly down at Fawn. "You're damn lucky I stumbled along tonight. Don't get your hopes up that I've been hanging around all these years for you to come back, Fawn. You're just a pleasant memory to me. I've saved many a damsel from the clutches of Stanley Fulbright. You're just one more."

He strode toward the door and was startled when he felt Fawn's feathery touch on his arm. For an instant, he thought he'd go mad from the physical restraint he forced upon his body.

"What?" he snapped.

Fawn swallowed her pride. "I'm sorry I misjudged

you, Garrett. And thank you for taking care of Stanley." She lowered her eyes so she wouldn't have to stare into the penetrating glare of a man who could devour a woman with one swift glance. Sparks of desire were rising within her.

"Give my best to Marcy Ann." The very name cooled her weakness for Garrett.

Chapter 5

Fawn eased her father's truck onto the rough gravel road lined with jack pines and wilted goldenrod. The smell of rain still clung to the air as the morning sun began to burn off the fog. She'd borrowed the truck after finding Garrett's coon hounds sniffing around her mother's French poodle. A twinge of remorse again drifted into her consciousness.

She'd accused Garrett of waiting at the cabin to see her. She battled disappointment at discovering the truth. Garrett never intended on seeing her. After all, he was with Marcy Ann now. Perhaps this was a sign she should get on with her life.

The Horton farm came into view. It was an old farm house that had been added on to several times as the kids were growing up. A long front porch with a swing at each end and flower planters still overflowing with sweet potato vine rested near the front door. Mismatched flower pots dotted the steps. Bluebird houses hung on the fence posts around the nearby pasture. Garrett's mom Sarah loved wild birds. She would find a new design every year in the magazine *Missouri Conservationist* for her husband to make. He never refused.

Fawn spotted the freshly painted red barn she and Kathleena had played in as children. They had often hid there to avoid babysitting Kathleena's twin brothers. Although they were cute, their mischievous antics wore thin after only a few minutes. Garrett would relieve them of their duty by taking the rowdy duo with him to work the farm. He had been so much more mature, even as a boy, Fawn realized.

She stopped the truck and tapped the horn lightly. A man with thinning gray hair and a thick speckled beard lumbered out onto the porch as he pulled on a blue jeans jacket.

Fawn opened the door and tugged on the leash secured to the dogs' collars. "Come on, boys. Out you go."

"As I live and breathe." The man moved off the porch and circled Fawn's waist with a bear hug. "It's my other daughter come home. Sarah, look who's here."

"Hello, Jessie." She placed a grateful kiss on his cheek. Why did all these warm feelings have to keep getting in the way of her hate for Westfork? Poor old Jessie, so gruff, so kind. He had been the understanding father she had always wanted.

"Let me look at you." Jessie twirled her around and whistled, so characteristic of his own wolfish son. "Prettiest girl in Iron County."

"I always did love you, Jessie Horton."

Fawn laughed as she spied Sarah standing at the screen door, wiping her hands on her soiled apron. A warm and tender smile spread across her lips and something else. Was it hope? Fawn wasn't ready to explore the option. She had the inkling that Sarah and her mother had shared intimate words about their children on Old Miners' Day.

"Mornin', Fawn. What brings you out so early?" Jesse took the dogs as she started up the porch steps.

The screen door slammed behind Sarah. Wiping her hands on a stained apron, she held up a cheek for Fawn to kiss. "Come inside. Jessie started a fire this morning and the house is hotter than a firecracker. Had to open the front door and several windows to cool off."

The house was still toasty warm from the cast iron stove in one corner of the living room. A picture of Jesus hung nearby, as did pictures of all her children. There was even one of herself and Kathleena when they were children. "Home," she whispered reverently.

Sarah slipped an arm around her shoulders. "This will always be your home if you want, Jeanie Fawn. You're like my own daughter. Heaven knows how I miss

Kathleena. Can you believe her running off and livin' with a bunch of half-wild Indians? Garrett says she's fallen for some rancher out there."

A laugh escaped Fawn. "Garrett checked him out, I suppose. From what I hear that wild Indian has more money than my dad."

Jessie joined them then forced Fawn down into a kitchen chair as Sarah began pouring three cups of coffee. "Sure. Took that city fella with him, too."

"Jerod?" Fawn failed to hold back the laughter. Jerod had been a photo journalist that had taken an interest in Kathleena. He didn't seem like the kind of man Garrett would approve of seeing his sister. "How did they get along?"

"You know Garrett," Jessie chuckled as he tried the hot coffee. "The Lord Almighty wouldn't be good enough for his sister. He let that Indian fella give him the boot. Kathleena has met her match there."

Fawn looked over the edge of her cup with a smile. "Sounds like Garrett is going soft."

Jessie winked at her. "Got woman trouble of his own, I think."

Fawn felt her face redden as everyone seemed to be staring into the depths of their black coffee. Startled at the slam of the front screen door, Fawn watched as little feet burst into the kitchen.

It was Joey Davies, Marcy's little boy. "Grandma Sarah!"

Sarah could not hide the look of panic that leaped into her eyes as she looked past Fawn into the living room. She pulled the little boy into her lap and gave him a squeeze.

The little boy then realized his teacher sat at the table. "Miss Turnbough!" He jumped down from Sarah's lap and ran to her. Fawn couldn't resist giving him a hug. "What are you doing here? Do you know my Grandma Sarah?"

Fawn tousled his hair with her hand and smiled. "I sure do. We're old friends."

Before she could comment further, another voice came through the front door. Her spine stiffened as the heavy steps of cowboy boots neared.

"Dad, who found my dogs?" Garrett's eyes then fell on Fawn sitting next to his mother.

"Look, Garrett," Joey said. "This is my teacher."

"I know. Nice to see you, Fawn."

Joey gave an unexpected hug to Fawn's neck then ran out the back door. "Are those kittens still in the barn, Grandpa?"

"Yep. Think I'll join ya." Jessie stood up and headed toward the door. "Don't be a stranger, Fawn. We've missed you something awful."

Fawn nodded a weak smile as he left. "I've got to be going. Told Dad I'd have his truck back before noon. Wants to get the oil changed."

"Don't leave on my account." Fawn couldn't decide

if Garrett was mocking her or being cruel. "It's just like old times seeing you sit at the breakfast table with Mom."

Sarah leveled a warning look at her son as she started to clear the table. "You come back real soon, sweetie." She blew Fawn a kiss then turned away.

Coming to the Hortons' had been a mistake. Her whole life this kitchen had been where she escaped for a taste of a normal family. No talk of mining lead here. With all the riches her family bestowed upon her, it was here that she wanted to be. She didn't care if the china matched or if the silverware had seen better days. The red checkered curtains lifting at the windows and the smell of apple pie in the oven spoke of coming home.

As she rose from the chair, Garrett shifted his weight to one leg. He dug his large tan hands deep into the pockets of his faded blue jeans. His cynical smile and lusty eyes did not belong to the same gentleman she'd seen the night before. Fawn frowned up at Garrett as she tried to pass him in the doorway.

She swallowed hard as she tried to look up at him with contempt. She felt his hand on her arm just as Marcy Ann came through the back door. The agonizing look of pain that filled the woman's eyes faded to anger.

"Thanks, Sarah." Fawn rushed out through the front of the house. When the screen door slammed, she started to walk faster. She heard the screech of the front door, then the slam. In seconds, Garrett was walking at her side.

He seemed to be amused at Fawn's nervousness. "Where were the dogs?"

"My mother's poodle is in heat. When I went to the house this morning, they were causing quite a commotion. My mother said if her dog is in the family way she'll personally shoot those over grown puppies of yours next time they cross her path."

Laughter was Garrett's response as Fawn continued her fast pace toward the truck. "Nell always was good for a laugh. Tell her I'll drop by and apologize in person."

Fawn didn't feel amused, not with Marcy Ann coming out onto the porch and staring a hole in her chest. She jerked the truck door open. "Tell her yourself!" she snapped. "You're still a public nuisance, Garrett Horton." She pulled herself into the truck and reached for the door handle. "Now if you don't mind, get out of my way."

She turned on the ignition and backed around in a huff. When she put it in drive, Garrett had planted his feet in her way. She wasn't very good at driving her father's stick shift and managed to kill the engine. It was long enough for Garrett to come along side and reach in to take the keys.

He leaned in the window and eyed her with less amusement now. His blue eyes examined her profile as she stared out the windshield as if he weren't there. "Why in such a hurry?" His voice was low and edged with a callousness. "The folks are tickled to have you here again. Which, by the way, is where you belong."

Fawn turned on him viciously. "How would you know where I belong? You're the reason I left." She grabbed at the keys dangling from his lifted index finger, which he snatched away. "Give them to me."

"I wouldn't want you running over me." He smiled coyly. "You certainly are in a mood this morning. I don't remember you being such a bobcat in the mornings."

"Just let me go or I'll—"

Garrett reached in and replaced the key in the ignition. "Or what? You'll hurt me with your little tantrums? Tell your daddy what a jerk I am?"

"I'm sure he already is well aware of that." Fawn took a deep breath then let it out slowly as her eyes shifted to Garrett. "You're a fool, Garrett Horton."

"Why do you hate me so much, Fawn? Last night you were ready to throw yourself at me."

"You always were full of yourself. It must be pretty difficult for you to realize that someone with a little class might just be appreciative of a late night rescue."

"As I remember, you used to like that side of me pretty well." He grinned. "Last night you thought I was a knight in shining armor."

"And today I see you for the court jester that you are. Now get out of my way." Fawn gripped the steering wheel with both hands and focused her eyes out the windshield toward Marcy Ann who had started down the steps.

Gently, Garrett took Fawn's stubborn chin in his

hand and forced her to look at him. For a moment, he drank in the beauty of her soft skin, the shine on her brown hair, and even the fire dancing in her usually tranquil doe eyes. "I didn't want your gratitude, Fawn," he said, his voice growing warm and even.

Fawn jerked her face from his hand. "I know what you want, Garrett, and you'll never get it. Not now or ever."

She turned the ignition and this time Garrett didn't try to stop her. She revved the engine and peeled out, throwing up gravel. Daring to look in her rearview mirror, Fawn's heart twisted at seeing Garrett still standing like a solitary oak, watching her as if she were a child having a temper tantrum.

He'd won again by forcing her into a battle of words. Garrett was a pro at wreaking havoc on a woman's senses. With gritted teeth, Fawn vowed never to succumb to that scoundrel's charm.

Chapter 6

"The way you're slamming doors and stomping through the house, I'd say something or someone has put a bee in your bonnet." Jim Turnbough's voice ricocheted in the main hall of his Southern-style mansion. It troubled him to see his daughter so unhappy these last few months. He knew it had something to do with Garrett Horton. "Want to tell your daddy about it?"

"No." Fawn hadn't meant to be snappy as she jerked on her black leather bomber jacket.

Jim reached out and grabbed her arm as she tried to push past him. "Hold on." His voice boomed in the two story foyer. "You've been in a lather all day. Was Jessie rude to my baby girl this morning?"

Fawn knew better than to try to shake her father off

as she'd done with Garrett. He would just love to turn her across his knee for a little taste of discipline. "Of course not," she said through gritted teeth.

He wanted an excuse to fire the upstart. "Then it was Garrett. What'd he do?"

Fawn threw her hands up in the air. "He exists, Dad. Isn't that enough? I loathe that pig. I hate him."

"Me thinks she protests too much," came a soft Ozark voice from behind her.

Whirling around to see her mother, Fawn shivered at the sensation of being caught red handed at lying. "Mother, don't play cupid with me." Her mother could be exasperating when it came to the affairs of the heart.

Her mother stepped forward and pushed Fawn's hair away from her face. "Garrett still loves you, sweetie."

"He loves Turnbough Lead, not me. Right, Dad?"

"Damned if I know, Fawn."

"Ha. Well, that's what you used to tell me a hundred times a day. Think that's changed? Every time we meet, I see dollar signs ring up in his eyes."

Nell sighed as she patted Fawn's shoulder. "Maybe that's just love shining through."

Fawn rolled her eyes upward. "You're a hopeless romantic, Mother. I don't believe in all that nonsense anymore. Love has never really worked out for me. Garrett betrayed my love a long time ago and I'm not giving him another chance to do it again."

"How, honey? You've never told us."

Fawn cast a guilty glance at her father, for he knew. Thanks to him, she hadn't made a total fool out of herself all those years ago. "I'm going to the cabin."

Nell frowned, disappointed. "I thought you were going to the club with us for dinner."

"Sorry. Another time." Fawn placed an affectionate kiss on her mother's cheek then embraced her father before rushing out to her Porsche.

The late afternoon sky was a brilliant turquoise, thanks to the rain the night before. A breeze swayed the stiffening leaves ablaze with color. Although muddy, Fawn decided to plant the bulbs she'd bought at the hardware store several days earlier. She imagined the tulips and daffodils bursting forth in the spring around the front porch of the cabin. The October sun warmed her back as she worked, helping her to forget the trouble that brewed inside her.

Living here, out away from people, was such a balm to her soul. When she felt overwhelmed or depressed, all it took was a walk along the creek or a stroll through the nearby woods. The meadows told the time of year by the wildflowers that bloomed. There were no highway sounds, or train whistles, no call for children to come wash for supper, or even the three o'clock pop of explosives detonating underground.

A peace filled her life when she was here among the woods. She had to admit that returning to Westfork for the most part had been a good decision, too. Everyone you met on the street was a friend or familiar enough to exchange greetings. A small-town warmth of friendship had folded her up in its traditions from the moment she'd arrived. There might be some gossip or speculation as to the reason for her return, but it was obvious the town embraced it lovingly. The feeling of being home filled a yearning and emptiness that haunted her for the last ten years. All that had evaporated when she caved to the acceptance that she loved the Ozarks.

Seeing Jessie and Sarah sipping coffee at their table had made her realize something else. She still wanted them in her life even if it meant running into Garrett from time to time. They were an extension of her family. Because of them, she'd learned how to do without gracefully in tough times. They were a proud people who didn't mind hard work or getting their hands dirty. Their love was boundless even though she'd abandoned them after the breakup that shamed Garrett.

It would be perfect if not for the marred picture of Garrett showing up from time to time. Somewhere in the back of her mind, a familiar echo began to haunt her. '*It isn't your gratitude I want.*'

Besides Turnbough Lead, just what did Garrett want? That old gnawing, like hunger, surfaced deep within the pit of her stomach, desiring something dangerous and exciting. Fawn shut her eyes against the image of Garrett reaching out to her in the still of the night.

She moved to the top step of her porch and surveyed

the land before her. "I will be careful this time," she vowed.

She wasn't sure what the cautious promise would entail, but the thought of resisting Garrett was beginning to soften what she thought was a heart made of lead.

∽∂∽

November came and went with only a few brief encounters with Garrett. Those few times were at church or in the grocery store. Marcy Ann and Joey dominated his attention. Fawn wasn't sure he had even been aware of her presence. Thanksgiving had been spent quietly at home with her parents. A few invited guests from out of town added a layer of safety Fawn craved

By the middle of December, Fawn received a letter from Kathleena, Garrett's sister. She would be arriving home with her new husband and adopted daughter. The letter had been full of excitement and joy with the insistence that Fawn attend Christmas dinner like the old days. Fawn had decided being with Kathleena and her new family was far too tempting an offer to resist. A few hours spent in the company of Garrett and Marcy Ann couldn't dampen a reunion with her best friend.

Fawn laughed as Kathleena swung open the front door of her parents' home. "Merry Christmas!"

"Fawn. It's been forever." Kathleena smothered Fawn with a hug and kisses on both cheeks. "You look amazing. What have you done to yourself? This country air agrees with you."

Fawn immediately spied the new husband in the corner, talking to Garrett and Jessie. He was just shy of six foot and very dark skinned. There was no hiding his Indian blood or the wickedness in his dark eyes as they fell on Kathleena. The love that passed between them made Fawn a little more than envious.

After introductions were made, Kathleena's husband, Caleb, continued to smile at Fawn. Kathleena had gone to check on her little daughter who'd gone down for a nap. Garrett left for more wood.

Caleb took a sip of the eggnog Sarah had forced upon him. "I feel as if we have known each other for many years, Fawn."

Fawn felt shy under the gaze of his penetrating dark eyes. "Don't believe everything Kathleena has told you about me."

"It wasn't Kathleena who talked about you, but Garrett."

"Garrett?"

"Yes. Last summer when we would ride over my land, Garrett spoke often of you. Said he wanted to bring you to visit next summer."

Fawn tried a light-hearted laugh. She knew it sounded fake. "I think you have me mixed up with his fiancée, Marcy Davies."

Caleb eyed Fawn with amusement. "Ah, maybe so.

Here's Garrett now. Let me help you with that."

He reached out to relieve him of some of the oak logs Garrett had brought inside off the porch. Garrett nodded thanks.

Garrett stoked the fire before standing to face Fawn. "The women get colder than a January blizzard. I'm ready to melt in here."

Fawn backed toward the kitchen to put more space between her and Garrett, who didn't shy away from appraising her body. A friendly smile spread across his wide mouth as he took several long strides toward her. Fawn's body was powerless to move as Garrett stopped in front of her. He lifted his eyes to something hanging over their heads.

"Mistletoe."

Before Fawn could side step him, Garrett pulled her into his arms, encircling her waist with his hands. For a second, he let his eyes swallow her beauty in great gulps. The feel of her silk blouse pressed against his chest. The leather pants she wore grew restrictive as her heat penetrated to his skin. He paused to savor the sensation for a few seconds longer before lowering his mouth to capture Fawn's trembling lips.

Taken by surprise, he felt Fawn begin to respond to the warmth flowing between them. Too quickly, he found he had released Fawn. She stood battling some internal conflict revealed in her light brown eyes. A rosy glow began to creep up her face.

"Merry Christmas, Fawn. We're all so glad you decided to come be with us."

"T—thank you, G—Garrett," she stammered. She tried to divert her eyes to the floor to hide what she feared would be an obvious glow. "I wouldn't have missed being with Kathleena for the world."

The words washed over Garrett like a cold glass of water. The joy of the moment vaporized as quickly as it had come.

Caleb chuckled, watching the two. "It makes my day to see a woman put your over-blown ego in place, Garrett." He winked at Fawn. "Now you know how your sister forced me into this marriage. I never had a chance."

Garrett tried to sound glib. "I knew you were doomed the first time we met." He jabbed his new brother-in-law as he joined him at the wood stove. His eyes went back to Fawn who watched the two mock each other. "Kathleena and Fawn are two women that will make a man lose all self-respect if given half a chance."

Caleb narrowed his almond-shaped eyes at Fawn and smiled. "Well done, Fawn."

The evening progressed with walks down memory lane, hot apple cider, and laughter. Fawn bathed in the glow of being home with the people she loved. Watching Kathleena's little daughter Raven turned out to be very entertaining with her boundless energy and adoring affection for Garrett. His charm wasn't lost even on a younger female.

Sarah's dinner of turkey, dressing, and candied sweet potatoes was perfection. Homemade cranberry sauce, green beans, and cornbread made everyone push away from the table with complaints of having eaten too much. However, after dishes were cleared, washed, and tucked away in glass front cupboards, Sarah brought out the three pecan pies and a red velvet cake. The twins, now high school juniors, ate several servings. The women ate a sliver of everything while the men complained Sarah must be trying to tell them something with the small slice they were served.

Darkness had fallen by the time the family filled up the small living room, the youngest members sitting on the floor near the Christmas tree. Little Raven helped pass out the gifts with the help of the twins. She was very pleased with herself at being able to help.

Sarah and Kathleena had both surprised Fawn with a special gift: a Lone Star quilt made by Sarah's own hands and a turquoise pair of earrings Kathleena had bought from a Navajo friend. Fawn knew this might happen and was prepared with gifts of her own. The twins got gift certificates to Bass Pro and the men new tackle boxes. She'd found a lacey shawl for Sarah and a pair of leather boots for Kathleena. Little Raven waited patiently for her gift that turned out to be a box of colorful books.

Paper and ribbon covered the floor. Laughter filled the room like a warm blanket. Fawn felt happier than she'd been in months.

Why hadn't she come home sooner?

Raven chose a book for Fawn to read to her. She crawled up in Fawn's lap and they snuggled together on the couch as quiet small talk began filling the room. When Raven began to yawn, Fawn kissed her on the temple.

"I have one more surprise for you, Raven." Fawn pushed the little girl to the floor as she took her hand. "Close your eyes." She couldn't help but laugh as the little girl's eyes clamped shut. "Okay, keep them closed. I'm going to lead you to the surprise. No peeking."

"Okay, Aunt Fawn."

The term of family connection touched her so suddenly Fawn wasn't sure she could speak. Fawn opened the door. "Okay, Raven. Open your eyes."

Raven opened her eyes and began jumping up and down as she pointed outside. "Look! It's snowing. It's snowing! Santa will come now."

Everyone raced to the windows and door to glimpse the glistening first snow of the season. The large flakes were falling fast.

The ground was already covered with more than an inch of powder. It was magical how everything looked flawless beneath the white cover of winter.

"I wanna go out," Raven begged Kathleena.

"Me too," Fawn cheered.

Kathleena laughed, scooping up the little girl into her arms. "Me too."

Garrett smirked and slapped his hands together. "Hell, me too."

In moments, the Hortons had poured outside into the yard, slipping and sliding around with feeble attempts to make snowballs that fell apart before they could be hurled. It didn't take long for the women to get cold and retreat back into the house. The men soon followed, moaning that the fun had just begun.

"I really must be going, Kathleena." Fawn slipped on her fur coat. "It's been wonderful seeing you. Your little family is amazing. I adore Caleb."

Kathleena couldn't resist shifting her eyes to her husband whose adoring eyes were upon her. "He is Mr. Right, Fawn. I love him so much." Tears formed at the edge of her eyes. "And Raven is my heart." She embraced Fawn. "Oh, Fawn, I see you and Garrett have not mended whatever happened between you so long ago. Don't let him marry that Davies woman. I couldn't bare it."

Fawn kissed Kathleena on the cheek. "By the way, why isn't she here?" The thought of her showing up had been a concern all evening.

Kathleena hooked her arm through Fawn's. "Her mother was celebrating Christmas tonight too. Lucky us." She lowered her voice. "Garrett refused to go because you were coming."

Fawn pinched Kathleena on the backside. "Stop it. You know as well as I do your mother would have had a stroke if all of us hadn't been together."

"You see? You just admitted we all belong together. Give Garrett a chance. I know he's a rascal, but deep down Garrett is a knight in shining armor."

Garrett chose that moment to join them. He slipped an arm around Kathleena and pulled her up tightly against his side before kissing her roughly on the cheek. "Singing my praises again, Kathleena?"

"Someone needs to," Fawn chirped sarcastically with a playful smirk. "You're lucky you have such a fan club."

"Better join up while the membership fee is cheap." Garrett gave his sister a wink before turning his blue eyes on Fawn. "Come June, I'm a goner."

Fawn remembered the wedding plans. "Come June, this world will be a safer place."

Garrett's smiled began to fade at Fawn's flippant comment.

She wasn't a wide-eyed innocent anymore. He couldn't push her to bend to his will. Now she was a woman of the world with a grasp of what she wanted. Only Fawn didn't seem to want the same thing he did.

"Tell you what, why don't you let me drive you home in that little hotrod of yours so I won't worry about you driving off some bluff?"

Fawn dared to smile coyly. "That would certainly put a crimp in your future plans, wouldn't it?"

Garrett released Kathleena and lifted his down jacket from the hall tree. "It most certainly would, Fawn."

Caleb joined them and pulled Kathleena into an embrace. "We'll be along in Jessie's truck to bring you back, Garrett."

Chapter 7

Garrett agreed to Caleb's suggestion and ushered Fawn out the door by taking her elbow. He managed to help her into the car before losing his footing and sprawling face down in the snow. When he cautiously made his way into the driver's side, Garrett frowned at the laughter that greeted him.

"Very funny."

Fawn's response was more laughter, which he didn't appear to mind after a minute or two.

The roads were slippery in spots but not treacherous. It wouldn't take long, as fast as the snow was falling. Highway crews would want to put off getting out the snowplows as long as possible, considering it was Christmas. Garrett appeared to be deep in thought as he carefully navigated the winding roads toward Pucky Huddle Hill.

"Kats looks good, doesn't she?"

The comment was so off-handed and friendly that it caught Fawn by surprise. "So in love. Who would've thought anyone would have ever captured that wild heart of hers."

"I saw the chemistry between those two last summer. They pretended not to notice each other, but heaven and earth couldn't keep them apart for more than ten seconds."

"I'm glad. She deserves the best."

Garrett glanced over at her. "And what about you? Don't you ever get lonely way out there in the sticks?"

"I'm minutes from Dad's."

"I don't mean 'Dad's.' I worry about you staying so much to yourself."

Fawn felt the hairs on the back of her neck stand up in warning. He was putting the moves on her again. "I find my company very refreshing."

Garrett chuckled deep in his throat. "Well, there doesn't seem to be any men coming around since Stanley Fulbright had a change of heart."

Fawn frowned. It was true. She had not even been asked to dinner since Stanley tucked his tail and ran off after Garrett's threats. "Do I have you to thank for that?"

"No. But I'm not beneath scaring a potential beau off if I thought you were in the least bit interested."

"You really are revolting, Garrett. How does Marcy Ann stomach you?"

"The same way you used to," Garrett quipped.

The Turnbough mansion came into view as Garrett killed the engine. He turned to face Fawn. He waited for her to turn her hardening glare toward him.

"Take me home, Garrett." Her voice matched the icy flakes that began to cloak the hood. "Or does your relationship to Marcy Ann mean so little to you that you'd throw yourself at me, knowing I loathe you?"

Garrett smirked as he reached out and toyed with the brown strands of Fawn's hair clinging to the rich white fur of her coat.

Startled, Fawn fell against the door. "Keep your hands to yourself."

"Don't you know how difficult that is, Fawn? You're driving me crazy with your cold silent treatment. Have you become so calloused and numb that your body no longer needs the warmth of another's love?"

"I have you to thank for that. All you have ever wanted was my father's company."

"Is that why you left?" he blasted. "You knew that from the start. I never lied to you about having big plans for Turnbough Lead."

She pulled the fur up around her neck. "You lied about loving me so you could have it."

"I suppose your dear old daddy did something to convince you of that." Garrett had always suspected Jim of sabotaging their marriage plans. The old man never wanted Fawn to marry a country boy with big ideas, especially if those ideas involved his lead mines.

Garrett sighed as his eyes caressed Fawn crouched against the door like a frightened animal. Gently, he pulled her resistant body into his arms. His voice was a whisper. "I won't hurt you, Fawn. You were the one special moment in my life. I'll never forget that even when I marry someone else. What we had together made me what I am today."

Fawn felt powerless when Garrett's breath touched her lips. Her body warmed to a rising passion she'd known only with him. The tug of his embrace melted the remaining resistance. Her eyes recognized the desire in his deep blue eyes.

"Leave me alone."

The protest sounded ridiculous even to her. There was no strength in her words. She felt Garrett's hand slip to the back of her neck and pull her forward into his body. Their mouths seared with lost desire and the lightning of forgotten love.

Garrett kissed her face and neck with urgency. "I can't let you alone, Fawn. I've got you under my skin. God help me, because I don't want this. I've tried to put you out of my mind all these years, but you're a ghost that won't go away."

Just as quickly as he'd taken her, Garrett released Fawn and started the engine. "I better take you on up to the house." His voice sounded far away and unsure. "Five more minutes and I'll lose all control."

Fawn didn't protest. Her behavior had been despicable and weak. Garrett had just made it perfectly clear her body still interested him. Any love he once had was dead. Something cried out in pain deep inside her. For a moment, Fawn had let herself believe that the longing in Garrett's eyes and the desire welling up between them had reawakened a buried love. She would just have to live with the knowledge that she still loved the devil in blue jeans. The fire burning inside her would be her demise if she didn't tread lightly.

The car inched forward to avoid sliding into the split rail fence lining both sides of the narrow road. Their breath seemed to crystalize in the silence that hung between the two former lovers. The hum of the engine failed to block out the racing heartbeats in their own ears. Garrett used the garage door opener then pulled in the Porsche.

Fawn's hands shook as she tried to unfasten the seatbelt. Garrett opened her door and finished the job as he helped her out of the car. They linked arms as they made their way to the backdoor of the Turnbough home. The electric candles glowed in each window, forming haloes against the moisture laden panes of glass. White Christmas lights twinkled in the trees and shrubs giving the falling snow an air of magic.

In the distance, another vehicle puttered up the hill.

Fawn guessed it would be Garrett's ride.

She paused before stepping up on the veranda that spanned the back of the house. "Thank you, Garrett, for driving me home. Again you have put on your suit of armor."

One corner of Garrett's mouth turned up in a smirk. "I like yours so well I thought I'd give mine a try."

Fawn's eyes widened in bewilderment. "What is that supposed to mean?"

For a moment, Garrett drank in the confusion brewing in Fawn's doe-shaped eyes. That had always been her best feature. They never ceased to amuse him when she'd ask him questions about life, smoking, drinking, and sex. Everything puzzled her and interested her at the same time. Riches had given her everything but experience. Only he had been able to give that to the poor little rich girl.

"Well?" A hint of spoiled impatience demanded an answer.

"It means that you have encased your heart so heavily in an invisible suit of armor that no emotion can possibly reach you." Garrett's eyes were drawn momentarily upward. The curtains to her parents' room pulled back slightly.

Fawn turned in a huff but not before Garrett pulled her back into his arms. "Not so fast." He reached up and pulled her face down to meet his. "Merry Christmas, Fawn."

He captured her mouth with his own burning kiss, taking the very breath from her. As she began to stir to desire once more, Garrett released her.

Pulling her coat tighter around her body, Fawn stomped away. "Merry Christmas, Garrett." With her head held high she rushed into the house.

His eyes once more traveled to the upstairs window and saw the curtain drop back into place. His smile broadened then he began to chuckle. He saluted the window with two fingers, before moving off toward the truck that had just arrived for him.

"I'll be back, old man. Count on that."

എഎഎ

The days of winter in the Ozarks could be harsh. The snow continued off and on for a week after the Christmas break. Roads were slippery enough that school was canceled until the second week of January. Temperatures dropped below zero several days. The wind chills caused the schools to shut down again because several frozen pipes burst.

But deep in the lead mines, the temperature remained a balmy sixty-five degrees. Garrett tried to stay below as much as possible since they were on a time crunch.

The flu had hit the men hard and tonnage goals weren't being met. That meant the new superintendent would be chewing him out or moving forward with the idea of reclaiming the high grade lead in the support pillars at the back of the mine. Garrett spent more and more time at the mine.

Marcy Ann had taken to questioning him about everything he did. Why was he late? Where was he going? Why couldn't he take more time for her? Why couldn't they go out? And on and on. She grated on his nerves more than the men who wanted a union, even more than the new superintendent, Tom Charleston. That was saying a lot. Garrett worked with the mine rescue team every week, came early, and stayed late. Then it was back to the mine to check on the night shift. Crashing on the couch in his office was easier than crawling into bed with a jealous woman.

He knew where the trouble rested. It started on Christmas when Marcy Ann found out that Fawn shared the holiday with his family. She exploded, saying Fawn was sneaking around behind her back to get Garrett in her clutches again. It didn't matter that he had reminded Marcy she had been invited but chose to go to her mother's. Apparently, that was beside the point. When she threatened to confront Fawn about the matter, Garrett informed her if she ever approached his former girlfriend about anything other than Joey's progress in school, he'd pack his bags and leave. She was just being ridiculous.

After that, their relationship began to deteriorate. There were tears for what Garrett thought was for no good reason. Complaints about everything from how to change a light bulb to how he brushed his teeth were common place. Then Marcy would swing the other way and be the angel he'd thought her to be a year earlier. He just never knew which Marcy was going to greet him when he came home.

Garrett realized one day that whatever feelings he thought he'd had for Marcy were dead. He had just put on his work boots and grabbed his hard hat when Marcy handed him a pan of freshly baked cinnamon rolls.

"What's this for?"

"I thought maybe some of the men would enjoy a treat. It's cold outside and this will make them think you're a rock star." She smiled and kissed him on the lips. "I love you Garrett Horton."

Garrett forced a smile, took the rolls, and left. He couldn't bring himself to say the words anymore. They were a lie. Two weeks later, he moved out.

Spring surfaced early in March. No one complained. It had been a bitter winter. Tonnage was up but the high grade lead that brought the highest dollar was in short supply. Big Jim had overruled Garrett's objections, stating that the overseas markets would soon have a glut of lead. Prices would fall and then he'd have to lay off people. Did he want that?

Garrett didn't have a choice. But he did have a choice in the pillars that were reclaimed in order for the mine to remain safe for his men. The extra work and concentration took his mind off Fawn.

Sometimes he'd see her going into church with her parents. He'd seen her coming out of the fire station with her kindergarten class but didn't want to stop because Joey would start asking questions. Marcy Ann thought they just needed some time apart and told Joey soon he'd have a new daddy. Garrett hated that she was using her son to make him feel committed to a relationship that no longer existed. As far as he knew, she had never approached Fawn.

The first of April Garrett rented a small apartment across from the bowling alley when things slowed down at work. The thought occurred to him that he might be wearing out his welcome sleeping on his best friend's couch. Shep Abney just grinned and said it was nice having the boss sleep over.

There wasn't much furniture. His mom let him take some old stuff from the barn that had belonged to her grandmother. He picked up some dishes at the Dollar General. The kitchen came with appliances so he didn't have to worry about a microwave. That would probably be the only thing he really needed, anyway. A few days later, Garrett invited the mine rescue team over to play poker. It was late when they left and he'd knocked back more beer than he normally would. Being in the apartment alone always made him realize something was missing in his life. He had already turned out the lights and striped down to his boxers when a light knock sounded on the door.

It was Marcy. "Hi, Garrett. Can I come in?"

Garrett eyed her and noticed she'd made an effort to look sexy. "Well, I donno, beautiful." His drunken smile and slurred speech made her laugh. "Why not? Get in here." Even before the door was shut, Marcy wrapped her arms around his chest and started kissing his neck.

They tangoed to the bedroom and fell across an unmade bed, laughing and pulling at each other's clothes.

Marcy kissed him passionately on the mouth and pulled away. "I'll be right back."

She disappeared into the bathroom to freshen up and finish removing her outer clothes. When she threw open the door and rushed to Garrett's side, she found him sprawled across the bed, dead to the world. No amount of shaking or teasing could wake him from his drunken sleep. With frustration, Marcy threw a pillow at him. It bounced off his head to the floor, causing him to roll to his side and begin snoring.

Garrett awoke that Saturday morning with a lulu of a headache. The smell of bacon cooking did nothing to soothe his sour stomach as he made his way to the small kitchen. Marcy Ann stood at the refrigerator in one of his shirts and a pair of his boxers.

He rubbed his head then his eyes to erase invisible cobwebs of confusion. "What are you doing here?"

Marcy chuckled. "As if you don't remember last night." She closed the refrigerator and walked over to Garrett. Wrapping her arms around him, she kissed him on the lips. "You still got it, baby." With that, she rubbed her hand across his buttocks and turned away to finish his breakfast.

Garrett frowned and flopped down in a wooden chair that had seen better days. "Got what? Nothing happened between us last night, Marcy."

"Afraid someone might find out we're still together." Her voice was taking on an edge of contempt.

"We're not still together, Marcy. I don't know why you're here but I think you should go. This isn't going to work out."

"Fine!" Marcy threw her spatula into the sink and stormed out. She retreated into the bedroom and, minutes later, he heard the front door slam.

He wondered why he'd ever taken an interest in the woman to begin with. He hadn't realized how desperate he'd been for companionship until that very moment. The image of Fawn began to form in his head—the way she smiled, the firmness of her lips, the earthy smell of her hair, and the sound of her voice when she laughed. There would never be anyone else for him.

He needed to convince her that she meant more to him than her father's mines. Whatever had spooked her to run away all those years ago needed to be addressed, and soon.

Chapter 8

Fawn inhaled deeply before taking a sip of her coffee. She stood on the front porch of her cabin, aware the smell of rain was in the air. The leaves of the trees had turned upside down, indicating a stormy day was ahead. She believed in those old wives tales connecting nature to life. Garrett's dad had filled her head with lore as she grew up. It was part of her past—the part she wanted to cling to like a life line. The morning sun streaked through billowing clouds and the wind began to move steadily through the tops of trees.

She couldn't help but remember how so many years ago a day just like this had been her undoing. It was prom day. Garrett had chosen her to take to the prom. She wasn't sure why. He teased her mercilessly along with his sister. The other girls in school had been crazy for him and Garrett never seemed to be without a girlfriend. But a few weeks before his senior prom he was once again free and wanted Fawn to be his date.

Fawn stood with her hands on her hips after she'd scampered down off the last of the hay bales in the Horton barn. "Me? Why me? Most of the time you're teasing me into tears or chasing me with a spider. I know too much about your mischief, Garrett Horton. If this is some kind of joke, I will tell your daddy."

She looked up at him with squinted eyes, trying to look tough. Even then, Fawn fought the urge to fling herself at him. Her love began the day he saved her from a runaway horse and protected her from an angry father.

Garrett looked over his shoulder, out the barn door, to make sure they were alone. He smiled coyly and took a step closer. She didn't retreat but held out her hand that pressed against his chest. "I want you to be my date. I'm a senior. I'm tired of messing around with these local girls."

"I'm a local girl." Fawn cocked her head and became aware Garrett was looking at her with interest. Something he'd never done before. "Don't you look at me with those bedroom eyes of yours, like I'm one of your cheerleader girlfriends."

Garrett chuckled and pushed her hand aside. He pulled her in his arms so fast that the cowboy hat resting on the back of Fawn's head fell off. "I want you to be my girl, Fawn. I've just been waiting for you to grow up a bit. You're such an innocent. Next year I'm off to college. I want to know you're here waiting for me. Don't want somebody with ambitions to put a move on you while I'm gone."

Fawn tried unsuccessfully to squirm away. His muscular arms tightened. She wanted to stomp on his foot, punch him in the ribs, or twist his ear like she'd done so many times before when he'd played a trick on her or jumped out to scare her in the woods.

But she couldn't. He was looking at her with amusement mixed with something else. "What are you talking about, Garrett?"

Before Fawn knew what was happening, Garrett had kissed her. It was short and sweet but it managed to steal her breath away. "You are the prettiest girl in the county, Fawn."

Fawn's eyes drifted to his full lips as a whisper escaped her mouth. "That would be your sister. They don't call me the 'Plain Jane' friend of the Horton clan for nothing."

"They're wrong. I'm done with the other girls, Fawn."

"I don't understand." Fawn knew she should try to escape his embrace but she loved standing pressed against his chest. "Stop teasing me, Garrett. You're going to hurt my feelings."

Garrett watched her lower lip push out. He reached

up and ran a finger over it before kissing it again. "I'm not teasing. From now on you're my girl."

"I—I—" Fawn felt his mouth on hers again. "Your girl?"

"Go with me to the prom."

Fawn nodded and smiled. She was a junior and had no prospects for a date. Kathleena enjoyed multiple offers. She had promised Fawn she would take her instead of one of the Westfork boys. Maybe that's why Garrett was asking her. "Did Kathleena put you up to this?"

Garrett smiled warmly. "No. But I did tell her what I was planning. I made her promise to convince you to go with me if you refused." He stepped back and took both her hands in his. "Fawn, I've been carrying a torch for you for some time. This isn't going to be a one night stand. It's you and me from now on."

Fawn pulled him back so that he stood inches from her. "Yes."

The next few weeks had been a whirlwind of prom dress shopping and trying to explain to her father why she was going to prom with that high and mighty Horton boy. Thanks to her mother, his objections didn't prevent her from being Garrett's date. A group of kids from school were going to Farmington for a late movie and ice cream after the prom ended at eleven. But Garrett and Fawn ended up at the cabin. Fawn now realized he wanted to make sure she would be his, mind, body, and soul before he went off to college in Rolla. Neither of them expected the explosion of passion that cemented their love.

Fawn shook her head free of the memories that felt like cobwebs forming over her common sense. A gust of wind dropped a branch in the nearby stand of trees, breaking her reflection of happier times. She walked inside the cabin to try to get the weather report on the radio. There was a severe thunderstorm watch out but Fawn wasn't too concerned. It would be hours before it reached this part of the state. But she knew things needed to be secured before that time.

By late afternoon, she had taken her two horses back to the small shed she'd turned into a barn. One mare would foal anytime. She made sure she was in the largest stall before leading the gelding into the narrow lean-to on the side of the shed. With the gate secured, the gelding grew more nervous and snorted his disapproval as Fawn turned to leave.

Even though she hated the partially buried storm shelter, Fawn opened the hatch door and took supplics down the three steps. Light flooded from above but she still needed a flashlight. She quickly turned it on to make sure spiders and other creatures hadn't taken up residence. After a thorough cleaning, she added a folding chair, even though there was a cement bench her father had made years ago. A couple of shelves held an LED lantern, a battery operated radio, and some bottled water. A first aid kit, a plastic container that held socks, a windbreaker, and a blanket sat safely on the lower shelf. Fawn shoved some granola bars and a bag of almonds in the box as a precaution, in case she had to come down for several hours.

By the time she'd decided to call it a day, the sky was darkening and the sound of her nervous horses forced her inside to listen to the radio again. It was nearing seven and there should have been another hour of light. Thunder rumbled down the valley as rain started to pelt through the window screens. Fawn lowered the windows and flinched as lightning struck somewhere in the woods. The wind howled, shaking the front door as Fawn decided to take a quick shower. She wondered if it were too late to try to make it to her parents' house.

※※※

The doorbell rang at the Turnbough mansion. Nell flung open the door and sucked in her breath. "Garrett!"

Garrett pushed inside, wiping the rain from his thick mane. "What's wrong?"

Big Jim entered the foyer as he put on his hat and rattled his keys. "What do you want?" he growled.

"I need to talk to Fawn. Is she here?"

"No." Nell grabbed Garrett's arm. "That girl is still at the cabin. Jim has tried to call her but she isn't answering her cell. The news on the TV just said a tornado touched down in Salem. It's headed this way. Oh, Garrett, I'm so scared."

Big Jim started to walk around him. "I'm going to get her now."

"You don't have a four-wheel drive. I do." Garrett opened the door. "Get Nell to the basement. The cell tower is probably out. It's hit or miss out there, anyway. The creeks are going to be rising soon if they aren't already. If I can get her out, I will. If not, we'll weather the storm there in the storm shelter." He turned to see Big Jim take hurried steps toward him. Garrett expected a confrontation. "Don't try and stop me, old man."

Big Jim frowned but reached out and clamped a large hand on Garrett's shoulder. "Take care of my girl, Garrett."

Garrett saw fear in his adversary. He nodded then turned back to kiss Nell on the cheek. "Get to the basement," he ordered.

She sniffed back a tear and pulled at her husband.

The storm intensified as Garrett neared the cabin. The creek was already starting over the low water bridge but he managed to navigate through. He could see lights in the cabin as he pulled to a stop near the porch steps. Once outside, he scrunched his shoulders against the blowing rain as he ran up the steps. The wind against the trees sounded like they were snapping like brittle twigs.

Garrett jerked the screen door open before pushing through the front door.

"Fawn!" he yelled as he rushed through the kitchen then to the bedroom.

She came running out of the bathroom smack into his arms. She wore a pair of faded jeans and a tee shirt, damp from not drying off. Her hair still dripped from her shower.

"We need to get to the shelter," he said.

She nodded as she slipped her feet into some sandals and let him pull her roughly to the door.

As they stepped on the porch steps, the sound of trees falling forced them to fight against the debris slapping at their bodies. Garrett forced the door of the shelter open against the wind so Fawn could slip down the steps. The door slammed behind him as he entered. Fawn had turned on the LED lantern as he struggled to bolt the door. He backed down the steps, watching the door as if it would fly open any second.

She circled his waist with one arm and pulled him back against the concrete bench. She buried her face in his back as the door rattled and strained against its hinges. Garrett turned and pulled Fawn down on the bench. He wrapped his arms around her and felt hers pull him close. Her cheek lay against his shoulder and her trembling body shuddered as the storm intensified, slamming objects against the door.

"You're freezing."

Garrett stood up and opened the plastic box. Pulling out the blanket, he wrapped it around Fawn's back, aware her bare skin was covered only with a thin tee shirt. He pulled her close and rubbed her back briskly. When her teeth began to chatter, Garrett forced her into his lap. He continued to massage her back and realized her breasts were pressed firmly against him. For the first time in his life, Garrett was paralyzed with fear of losing something he longed to possess.

"Don't be scared, Jeanie Fawn. I'm here."

Fawn stopped shivering, feeling the warmth of Garrett's body against hers. She realized then that he was also wet and probably cold. She made an effort to extend the blanket around him and found her face touching his. When she smiled, their lips touched. She reached up and moved a lock of hair the color of wet sand away from his forehead. His blue eyes penetrated her defenses as she acknowledged she felt joy sitting in his lap with his hand up the back of her shirt.

She placed her hands on each side of his face. He needed a shave. He continued to stare at her as she let her gaze explore his face as if seeing it for the first time. "I'm not scared of the storm. I'm afraid of what I want to do with you, Garrett."

Garrett captured her mouth with his own and kissed her long and hard. As his kisses started to trail down her jaw then to her throat, Fawn was keenly aware that his hands had found the sensitive spots that drove her into mindless submission. She could feel his body begin to demand more. She knew that Garrett had been the only man ever to bring her to the point of euphoria. No matter what he was in the light of day, tonight he was the knight in shining armor that would rescue her from the chains she'd bound around her heart. The fight now lived in the storm, not in the shelter where they began to rediscover a love turned to stone.

She was impatient to have him. But when the door of the shelter stopped rattling as quickly as it had started, Garrett pulled back. With gentle hands, he moved Fawn onto the bench before going up the steps and listening. He unlocked the door as Fawn joined him with the lantern. With care, he pushed open the door before taking the small lantern from her hands.

It continued to rain but it was light. The wind felt more like a breeze than a killer tornado. As they came up onto level ground, they spotted Garrett's truck. A small tree had crashed down on the bed but it didn't look as if it was destroyed. The cabin appeared to be still standing, as did the shed. Tree limbs were everywhere. Sounds of rushing water meant no one would be crossing the low-water bridge this night.

The sound of an anxious horse reached them.

"Something's wrong." Fawn tried to pick her way carefully through the debris to reach the shed.

Garrett grabbed her arm to make sure she didn't stumble. When he slid back the shed door, Fawn cried out. Her mare was in labor.

"Looks like we're having a baby." Garrett went into the stall and rubbed the mare's neck. "You're doing great, girl. Come closer, Fawn, so she can see you. Talk in a normal voice to calm her. This is her first. Right?"

Fawn nodded, knowing there wasn't much Garrett didn't know about her animals. She began to talk to the mare about the storm and about how proud she was of her for having a foal. At one point, Fawn tried to sing a silly song she used to call her students to story time each day. Garrett smiled and went to the back of the mare.

"Okay, ladies, I think we have a baby." The foal wiggled as the mare got to her feet and started licking her colt. Garrett was grinning ear to ear. "It's a boy. Do you have a name picked out or is it too soon?"

"How about Storm? It seems fitting." Fawn motioned for Garrett to follow her out of the stall. "He's beautiful."

"Handsome. Guys aren't pretty."

Fawn chuckled. "Spoken like a real redneck." Their eyes locked and they stood in silence, not sure of how to proceed. "It's starting to rain again. Please tell me we don't have to go back down in that cellar."

"Let's see if we can get a weather report from the radio. I want to make a sign and take it back down to the creek in case someone comes looking for us. I don't want them crossing that water. We'll wait it out until morning."

They entered the kitchen and soon realized the electric was out. He checked to see if the radio had batteries and was relieved that it could still pick up the station in another town. Garrett listened to reports coming in from

Potosi, Farmington, and Bismarck where the tornado had touched down. Westfork had suffered only minor wind damage.

Fawn kept markers and a white board at the cabin to try out lessons for her class. She wrote in large letters that they were safe before slipping the sign into a large, clear storage bag. "I think it will stay dry even if you puncture a hole in the back to hang it up."

Garrett took the board and kissed her on the mouth. "I'll be right back. Stay inside. Do you have another flashlight? I'll leave the lantern here."

She pulled out a drawer, handed him a small flashlight, and then watched him disappear out the door. The smell of the cellar, hay, and horse clung to her clothes. The clean tee shirt was now smudged with mud and stuck to her body. The jeans weren't in any better shape. Kicking off the sandals, she proceeded to pull off the tee shirt and cast it aside in the bedroom. The rest of her clothing slipped to the floor outside the bathroom as she hurried inside to get another shower. Since her gas water heater was still functioning, there was no shortage of hot water.

The soapy lather began to work its magic as she felt the shower curtain pull back. Water cascaded down her naked body as Garrett joined her. She'd forgotten how hard and handsome his physique was as he began rubbing the soap from her skin. Soon she had returned the favor by rubbing the lavender soap into his skin. She laughed, telling him he would be the best smelling miner at Turnbough Lead at this rate. After drying each other off, Garrett pulled her into the bedroom. The lantern rested in the bathroom, spilling only ribbons of light to shine against their bodies.

"I still want you, Fawn."

Fawn led him to the bed and backed him up so he had to sit down. "I know."

Chapter 9

Morning light brought another warm spring day. Birds had just started their wake up music when Garrett opened his eyes to stare into the face of his beloved, Fawn. She looked like the young girl he'd first made love to so many years ago. Her tawny hair, streaked with a mix of red and brown, drew his hands to remove the strands that fell across her cheek. She'd come to him so willing and passionate. The years of absence and pain faded away so quickly Garrett forgot she'd abandoned him. His broken heart had grown calloused and unforgiving over the years. It felt regenerated in dawn's new day.

He ran his hand over her bare shoulder then onto her back before pulling her into his embrace. There had been no hesitation in her love making. She'd remembered what he liked and brought him into submission several times before surrendering to his need to explore the love he once lost.

During the night, he'd gotten up and opened the windows to let the smell of rain fill the room. Then he'd stirred her to waken as he took her again. This time Garrett used a deliberate slow pace to lengthen her pleasure and his own.

Exhausted they'd fallen into a deep sleep.

Being an early riser, Garrett lay still as long as he could before slipping out of bed and into his clothes that still lay scattered near the bathroom door. He quietly left the cabin and went to check on the horses. He let the mare and her colt into the corral before releasing the gelding into the pasture. When he started back to the house, he saw Fawn walk out onto the porch with a look of concern.

"Think I took off?"

Garrett came up the steps two at a time and pulled Fawn into his arms. He kissed her mouth then her neck before running his hand down her backside. She had slipped on a long tee shirt and he realized it was his old football jersey from high school. Knowing she'd kept it all these years gave him hope.

Fawn smiled up at him as she circled his waist. "Maybe. I thought you might be afraid to try my coffee."

"You made coffee?" Garrett released her and opened

the screen door. "Wonders never cease. There's hope for you yet, Jeanie Fawn."

They brought their coffee outside to sit on the swing. Very few words passed between them as they listened to the sounds of nature. The sky was turning deep blue and the clouds seemed to disappear. It was as if no storm had ever occurred. When they did speak, it was about the new colt or fixing Garrett's truck. A familiarity formed between them that felt natural and right.

Garrett knew the subject of their future needed to be addressed. "Fawn, was last night just because you were scared and grateful, or was it something else?" Fawn looked down into her coffee cup to avoid looking into his eyes. Garrett reached out and lifted her chin with his finger. "I need to know. If you're hesitating because you think I'm still with Marcy Ann, I want you to know that was over several months ago. I moved out the end of January."

Fawn nodded. "I heard that you had." Her voice was so soft Garrett had to lean in to hear her. "We still have a lot of issues between us, Garrett."

"What issues? I don't care that you ran out on me two weeks before the wedding." His voice was sharp.

Fawn narrowed her doe shaped eyes. "Ran out on you?" She stood and walked to the screen door. "So this is all my fault? What about you marrying me for the company?"

Garrett jumped up off the swing and moved toward

her. "The company be dammed. Your old man has filled your head with so much prejudice against my family that you've come to believe we're just a bunch of rednecks and loggers who aren't good enough for your high and mighty ways." He was angry and dangerously close.

Fawn frowned at the insinuation. "I love your family."

"Funny how you can say you love my family but it kills you to admit you feel the same way about me."

"That's because I don't. You asked me about last night. Well, here is the truth. I wanted you. Period. I'm not proud of lusting after you. You were convenient and I have needs too."

"A shame Stanley Fulbright wasn't available."

"You're despicable, Garrett Horton." Fawn turned and stormed into the house. "The sooner you're gone, the better. I'll let you know when I need another roll in the hay," she confessed with thick sarcasm.

Garrett thought about going in after her. She was lying. He would wrap her in his arms again and make love to her until she admitted the truth. She loved him. The old Fawn would have bent to his will. This one could stand on her own two feet. He needed to tread lightly so as not to scare her off again. Whatever made her bolt ten years ago could happen just as easy this time. There was talk that her teacher contract might not be renewed due to cutbacks. He needed to cement their relationship before she started looking for a job in another town.

A horn started blowing as a truck appeared on the other side of the low water bridge. It was Shep Abney, his best friend. With careful forward motion, the truck made it through the waters that had begun to run clear again.

"Big Jim sent me to check on you." Shep got out of his truck and surveyed Garrett's truck. His eyes then drifted to the cabin. "Everything okay?"

"Not really. Just look at my truck," Garrett snarled as he walked down the steps.

Shep grinned and waved at Fawn who returned to the porch in a pair of blue jean cut offs and a blue tee shirt. "I wasn't talking about the truck, dumbass," he whispered. Shep whistled at Fawn. "Next time call me, Fawn, and I'll come save you."

Fawn joined them at the truck. She hugged Shep. "Deal. I'll be sure to let my dad know."

Shep pulled off the largest branches and nodded at the dents. "Not pretty but it should run. Just came by to see if you guys needed help in getting out. Things in town look a little windblown but not much damage. The Baptist church did get the cross on the steeple tipped on its side and the Dollar General got a window knocked out, thanks to a trash can going airborne. Several creeks got in some houses but other than that it's all good."

"And the school?" Fawn hoped nothing was amiss there.

"No problems." Shep turned back to Garrett. "Pumps

went out in the mines. Some flooding expected if the power doesn't come on soon. Big Jim is on his way. Thought you'd like to get in on that. I can take Fawn to her momma's."

Fawn frowned. The two talked as if she wasn't present. "I don't need you to take me anywhere, Shep. My car was in the garage and is just fine. I'll drive myself."

Garrett ignored Fawn's flippant remarks. "Let me get my wallet. I left it inside the house."

He entered the kitchen and found his wallet lying on the old cabinet Fawn loved so much. He picked up the flashlight from the table and opened the drawer where he'd seen Fawn get it the evening before to assist him in taking their sign to the creek. At first, he was stunned to see some pictures of himself. He laid the flashlight inside and pulled out the photos. He was naked with several girls either on him or in a similar state of carnal pleasure. Who were they and how old were the pictures? He flipped over the back and saw the stamped date. It was four weeks until his college graduation and three weeks from his wedding.

Shoving them inside his shirt, he closed the drawer and headed back outside. Shep and Fawn were talking about the storm.

"Let's see if this will start." Garrett jumped in the truck and had no problem turning it over.

He nodded to Shep who said his goodbyes to Fawn before getting in his own vehicle. Fawn turned her eyes on him in haughty contempt before walking away without a word. When she passed in front of his truck, he hit the horn making her jump. Garrett grinned at her angry glare. He backed the truck around and sped off. When he looked in the rearview mirror, Fawn was gone.

སྐ

Once at the mine, Garrett was geared up to be ready to go underground when the power surged to life at the mill. Several men stood around waiting as he walked up. He spotted Big Jim immediately and realized that, thanks to the mine superintendent Charleston, he might as well be invisible. Their heads were together, but it was the superintendent who talked, jabbing a finger into his clipboard as if by doing so would drive his point home. Garrett knew what that point was—mining pillars for bigger profits.

Charleston stood to gain a substantial bonus if he got his way. The miners doing the work would get an increase in profit sharing so there would be little grumbling overall.

But it was Garrett's job to make sure the men remained safe while they got the lead out. The superintendent wasn't a mine engineer like Garrett.

He was a geologist with a fancy degree from some school up north. He didn't have family in the area and felt no connection to the plight of his men trying to make a living. That was a dangerous combination.

Garrett pushed his way to the man's side. "How long before we have power, Jim?"

"Within the hour I'm told. Third shift is still down there. Pumps are down too." Big Jim puffed out the words in concern as his hands landed on his hips. "We're nearing that twelve hour mark."

Garrett knew that the sump would handle the water until then. After that, the water would start to flood the mine. "I'll get the mine rescue guys here in case we need to go in." He looked at his watch then lifted his cell phone to his ear. After calling his men, Garrett turned back to Jim and Charleston. "On their way."

"You're jumping the gun again, Horton." The superintendent wasn't timid at his rebuke as the other men strained to hear. "You're always trying to be the hero."

"Well, somebody has to have a little common sense," Garrett snapped.

"You're right about that. Where would you recommend I find a lead miner with some of that because it isn't you. Just because you strut around like you're god's gift to mining doesn't mean you know a damn thing."

"I can see why you'd think that since you're a gutless geologist who gets claustrophobic just going into the closet to get a change of clothes." Garrett smirked as he noticed the superintendent getting red in the face. "When was the last time you were underground?"

Jim stepped between the two men with a calm demeanor. "That's enough, Garrett. Show a little respect. The man's your boss." He nodded for him to move away and started to walk beside him.

"The man is an idiot," Garrett protested. "He doesn't care about these men. Was he trying to sell you on taking more pillars?" Jim just nodded and appeared unconcerned as he stared straight ahead. "That's insane. The mine will come crashing down. I know the market is falling but at some point, it will stop. Overseas markets in China are begging for the stuff. Just be patient, Jim. Trust me."

Jim stopped and took a deep breath. "We'll see."

"And your daughter is fine in case you were wondering," Garrett quipped.

Jim frowned at his mine captain. "Her momma called as soon as she got to the house. It seems she was in a lather about something. I don't guess you'd know anything about that."

Garrett tuned back to look at the head frame when he heard it rattle up with the first few men from below. "Power is on. I'll go check the pumps. And yeah, I got a pretty good idea why she's hot under the collar."

"Care to share with me?"

Garrett met the old man's eyes with vengeance. "Not yet. But when I know for sure, you'll be the first to know. Trust me."

Chapter 10

Fawn knew what the doctor in Farmington was going to say before he ever examined her. It'd been five weeks since her last cycle. She was pregnant. Every morning she threw up. When she got home from school, she took a two hour nap. Ice cream seemed to be her food of choice. One night of passion would now haunt her forever. But the thought of carrying a child, even Garrett's gave Fawn a feeling of delirious joy. She imagined what the child would look like. A boy might grow muscular and handsome like his father. A girl might favor her. It didn't matter. Being a mother had seemed out of reach for her.

Her thoughts drifted to Garrett. He would know he was the father. Should she tell him or let him figure it out all by himself? Not telling him meant another way to hurt him. That night in the cabin, making love throughout the night had made her realize he still had a hold on her heart. She loved him. But did he really love her as he claimed? He'd cheated on her just before they were to get married. Thanks to her father, she discovered the real Garrett Horton—a liar, cheater, and opportunist. He'd taken advantage of her innocence early on to make sure she loved no one else. Unfortunately, no one ever measured up to him even after he destroyed her confidence and faith in relationships.

Could they make it work? Was starting over even possible? Maybe she should give him another chance. They made a baby together. He deserved a second chance if he wanted it. People changed.

Fawn listened to the doctor with the good news. He wrote a prescription for prenatal vitamins before handing her a packet of reading material and suggested websites. With the next appointment scheduled, Fawn wondered if she glowed when she left the doctor's office. Not wanting to fill the prescription in Westfork, she opted to use the clinic's pharmacy.

She gave the pharmacy tech her prescription and wandered over to the aisle with baby supplies. A newborn hat caught her eye and she couldn't resist taking it to the counter to place with the vitamins.

"Fawn?"

Fawn whirled around and suddenly felt dizzy. She

tried to smile. "Marcy Ann. What a surprise. Caught me playing hooky."

"Well, everyone needs a mental health day from time to time." Marcy chuckled as she eyed her competition. The pharmacy tech called Marcy's name. Marcy took the small white bag and smirked at Fawn. "My prenatal vitamins."

Fawn paled. "You're pregnant?"

The tech returned and leaned over the counter. "Sorry, Ms. Turnbough. She got the last of the vitamins. So sorry." She handed the prescription back to Fawn. "We should get more in tomorrow. Should I call you?"

Marcy tilted her head at Fawn. The smile had disappeared.

Fawn shoved the paper in her purse. "No. Thank you."

"Would you still like the baby cap? It's so cute."

Fawn shook her head and started to walk off when Marcy came alongside her. "Guess we're in the same boat, Fawn."

"Congratulations, Marcy. I'm really happy for you. I mean it." Fawn turned away before she could see the smug look on Marcy's face fade into remorse.

Fawn hurried to her car and locked herself in before laying her head on the stirring wheel. She could feel her joy smash into great sorrow. She started to turn the rearview mirror when something caught her eye. A red pickup truck was pulling up to the front door of the clinic.

With the dent in the bed, there was no doubt of who drove in spite of a glare on the window. She quickly started up the Porsche and made her escape before Garrett could spot her.

The truth stung; Garrett Horton was still a liar and a cheat.

◈◈◈

Garrett slammed his fist into the hood of his truck. He'd driven to Rolla to get an estimate on the storm damage. It would be a good time to track down a faculty advisor for one of the fraternities he thought might be involved in taking the photos of him. The Greek letters were hanging on the wall over his head where he'd laid prone on the bed. He needed to get to the bottom of this, before he went to Fawn with the truth. It had Jim Turnbough written all over the conspiracy to sabotage their wedding. What had the old man told her? Showing these hideous shots of him would be enough but there had to be something else to make her run so far away and marry another man. He should have gone after her. But his wounded pride refused to be humiliated further.

The faculty advisor had died and a much younger man had taken his place. With a few calls, he tracked down one of the frat boys, now a Ph.D. at the university. He agreed to meet with Garrett. Fortunately, he remembered the event. He was told it had all been a joke to try to win a bet. If Garrett got drunk and crazy then the fraternity would get a nice little endowment and scholarship for their frat house. He mentioned a few names that Garrett remembered but had lost touch with over the years.

Driving the sixty miles back to Westfork, Garrett tried to decide what the best strategy would be to approach Fawn with this information. She would refuse to believe her father capable of such a despicable scheme. Jim ruined both their lives and futures because he feared losing the mines to a country boy with ambition. He would confront the old man with what he knew and see how things played out. Then he'd go see Fawn.

The memory of lying next to Fawn on a stormy night still haunted him. Making love to her made him realize how raw and empty his life had been since she left. For the first time in ten years, he felt whole. The first thought of the day was of her beautiful body wrapped in his. When he finally closed his eyes at night, he remembered the smell of her hair and the softness of her lips on his. It had been weeks since he'd seen her. Work had been brutal. He'd left her several voice mails but as of yet, had been ignored. Apparently, there was no limit to her contempt for him. Fawn no longer was a submissive, starry eyed girl who worshiped the ground he walked on. The fact she'd evolved into a beautiful, head strong woman who felt perfectly happy without him only made her more desirable.

The last of the day shift stepped off the head frame

cage into bright light. Reflex made them squint or shade their eyes as they made their way to the changing room where they'd shower the lead dust from their skin and change clothes before heading home. The routine made their wives happier. Although the lead dust posed no danger to their health until it had been smelted, coming home looking like they'd been rolling in a mud hole did. Garrett saluted several of the men, nodded to a few others as he grabbed his hard hat out of the truck. He could feel the pop, pop, pop of explosives underground and stood still for a few seconds to reassure himself all was well.

A smug grin started to form on his mouth as he imagined Big Jim exploding when he confronted him with the evidence he'd gathered earlier in the day. Garrett went straight to Jim's office and leaned in the doorway as he listened to the old man growl at someone on the other end of the phone. He slammed the receiver down and snarled at Garrett.

"Enjoy your day off? You know that was vacation, right?"

"It was worth it, Jim."

"You know you're the only one that calls me by my first name. Try calling me Mr. Turnbough for a change. I don't like your attitude much."

Garrett chuckled knowing he was about to drop a bomb on his boss. "Is there anything about me you do like?"

Big Jim looked at the phone then at him with a raised

eyebrow. "As a matter of fact, there is." He puffed out air as if he'd been holding it tight in his chest. "I like your work ethic. Nobody works as hard as you. I know when I say get the lead out, you'll do it faster, cheaper, and safer than anybody else."

Garrett straightened to his full height and cocked his head in suspicion. "Thanks. I guess."

"That's why I'm giving you a promotion."

Garrett narrowed his eyes. "To what? Head dog catcher in town?"

"No need to be a smartass, Garrett. I'm making you mine superintendent of the Bunker mine. Start tomorrow."

"What happened to Tom Gilliam? He's been there fifteen years."

"Retired."

"Since when," Garrett snapped. "He's one of the good guys. His family has worked in the mines ever since you dug the first shaft."

"I made him an offer he couldn't refuse. Out with the old, in with the new. Besides, you've been whining about a promotion for two years. Here's your chance to impress me."

Garrett took a step forward. "I don't give a damn if I impress you, Jim. All I care about is the truth. He took the pictures out of his shirt pocket and threw them on his desk. "What the hell did you do?"

The old man didn't even glance at the pictures. "I

heard you were asking questions around Rolla today."

Was there no place Jim Turnbough didn't have influence? "Is that why I suddenly got a promotion? You got rid of a man who knew more about mining than all of us put together and kept that worthless Charleston because you're afraid I'm going to tell your little girl what you did to break us up?"

Big Jim pooched out his lips and twisted them to the side before speaking. "You want the job or not?"

"You bet I do." Garrett grinned wickedly. "And the price?"

"Stay away from Fawn. Never speak of this—" He nodded toward the pictures. "—or I'll fire your sorry ass."

"You know what, Jim? I won't tell her. She already thinks I let her down. Finding out her father is a monster would be too much. Not to mention what it would do to your wife." His voice had taken on a lethal growl. "I plan to win Fawn back one good deed at a time. If it takes me another ten years, I'll do it. I've waited most of my life for the poor little rich girl. She loves me whether you approve or not. She just doesn't know it yet."

The old man jabbed a finger in Garrett's chest. "Job or Fawn? Which will it be?"

Garrett knocked the crooked finger away. "Tell the truth or let Fawn find her way back to me?" Garrett pointed to the pictures. "I have copies."

"Get out! Be at Bunker tomorrow morning at five

thirty before third shift leaves. You'll need to reassure them." Jim turned and went around his desk to stare out the window over the mine yard and out to the tailings pond.

Garrett wanted to go straight to Fawn and share about his promotion. It was what he'd wanted for as long as he could remember. Only in those dreams and plans, Fawn had always been a part of his life. With the things the way they were right now, she'd probably just insult him. He drove past the turn off to her cabin and wondered if she were home. It was after five. The Baptist church always had potluck dinners on Wednesday nights so she probably was with her mother preparing something to take. Turning the car around Garrett headed back to his apartment. It had been a long day. Tomorrow would be longer. He wanted to plan his reassurance speech for all three shifts. Miners were superstitious.

∽∾∽

Several weeks had passed since Fawn had watched Garrett pick Marcy up at the clinic in Farmington. The baby growing inside Fawn offered joy but also trepidation. Raising a child on your own was no easy task. She knew her mother would be beside herself whenever she got the courage to tell her. How could she remain in Westfork and be the butt of jokes and gossip concerning her child and Garrett?

It wouldn't be difficult to figure out the child's father.

Garrett cornered her outside the post office as she was coming out from mailing a package to his sister in Oklahoma. "Did your phone break, Jeanie Fawn, because I've left several messages for you?"

Fawn caught his earthy smell as his sky blue eyes melted her resistance. "No. Just ignored them."

She started around him nonchalantly. He followed her to the little Porsche and put his hand against the door so she couldn't open it.

"You in a hurry?"

Sighing Fawn turned to face him. "I hear congratulations are in order."

Garrett smiled proudly. "Yeah. Kind of surprised about the whole thing but I think it will work out."

Fawn frowned. "You've got it all figured out don't you, Garrett Horton?"

He took a step closer and drank in the softness of her skin and the shine on her hair. "You are still the prettiest girl I've ever known, Jeanie Fawn." His voice was low and sensual as his hand slipped into hers.

With a disgusted look at their hands, Fawn jerked free. "Stay away from me, Garrett. I can't believe you're standing here making a move on me after all you've done."

"What are you talking about? If you're referring to spending the night together—"

"Shush! Someone will hear you." Fawn looked around to see if anyone was listening but the parking lot was nearly empty. "I want to forget that night. We made a mistake. I made a mistake. I should never have fallen for all that country boy charm you're so good at spreading around."

Garrett opened the car door for her as she slid in. He could feel his temper rising. "I haven't been spreading any country charm around except with you."

A cynical laugh escaped her lips as the Porsche roared to life. "Whatever, Garrett." And she sped off, squealing her tires in the process.

Shep Abney drove up and stuck his head out the window. "Was that Fawn you were talking to?"

He nodded. "I get the feeling we were talking about two different things."

Chapter 11

"Did you hear Charleston and Big Jim got into it the other day?" Shep walked alongside Garrett as they headed to mine rescue practice. "Guess it was quite a shouting match."

Garrett entered the high school where they planned to go through some simulations. He'd come in earlier to set things up. "Over what? Who's the biggest dunderhead? Those two deserve each other."

"Not sure. Apparently, it had something to do with reclaiming those high-grade pillars."

Garrett stopped. "Do you mean to tell me that is still on the table? I made it very clear that was a disaster waiting to happen. Jim asked me to work up some specks on possible outcomes. Every one of them demonstrated the mine couldn't be supported with Charleston's plan. I thought Jim was on board with my findings."

Shep shrugged as he laid his gear down on one of the bleachers. "Donno." He smiled and cocked his head. "Maybe he misses you and Charleston is finally getting on his nerves."

"When hell freezes over." Garrett took a deep breath and tried to slow his heart rate down. He felt passionate about not reclaiming those pillars. "We have a meeting on Monday. I'll bring it up."

"Not to change the subject but have you talked to Fawn lately?" Shep tried to sound casual but couldn't pull it off.

"She ignores my calls so I stopped."

Shep busied himself with adjusting some of the equipment the team would use with the simulation. "Keep trying. I think you two should really give it a try."

Garrett frowned. "Since when did you start playing cupid? And now that I think about it, where have you been sneaking off to several nights a week? We used to play cards, coon hunt, and shoot pool at Murphy's. You work in town at the mine and I'm at the end of the world taking care of the Bunker outfit."

It was a few minutes before Shep answered. "Since you're such a big shot now, being a mine super and all I thought you might not want to hang around your uneducated buddy."

Garrett looked bewildered at his best friend and realized he was being flippant. "You've got more smarts than most people I know. Look at Charleston. He has two master's degrees and doesn't have enough sense to come in out of the rain." Garrett chuckled. "I think maybe you've got a girl." A slow wave of red started up Shep's face. He waved Garrett off. "I've never seen you blush before, Shep. Who is she? Do I know her?"

"I'm not ready to talk about it just yet, Garrett." He put his hands on his hips and dropped his head so that he stared at the gym floor.

"All right. All right." Garrett slapped him on the back. "You dog. We need to stay in touch better. When do I get to meet her?"

Shep started to speak but the rest of the team entered the gym, laughing and insulting each other. He smirked at his friend and nodded toward the others, signaling their conversation had ended. The thought of the shy Shep Abney having a serious girlfriend made Garrett envious. The guy clearly was in love. He'd never seen him so secretive and hesitant about sharing something that affected his life. It must really be serious, he decided or Shep would be blabbing like a gossipy old woman.

എഎ

Garrett sat down at the conference table in the administration building located just outside the gates of the Rocky Fork Mine. Being the first to arrive, he let his eyes drift out the large floor to ceiling windows to gaze at the Ozark hills. They were covered with blooming redbud and dogwood trees. Whether it had been the severe winter or the generous spring rains, they appeared more beautiful than in years past. He noted the sway of the jack pines near the tailings pond and remembered the weather forecast predicted another round of severe storms. The blue sky and warm temperatures lulled him into a false sense of security. He felt anxious to be back outside, enjoying the feel of the sun on his neck. Since things at the Bunker mine worked like a smooth running machine there would be no hurry to rush back after the meeting. Maybe he'd have lunch with the old Rocky Fork crew. Then again, maybe the storms would move in and he'd have to rescue Fawn again.

A sly smile began playing at the corners of his mouth as his thoughts relived the last time. No matter what words came out of her mouth, Garrett knew she still had feelings for him. It was there in the way she touched him and whispered against his mouth before begging him to take her again. The smile and sounds she'd made were all the same as before—before her father had destroyed the love between them. Anger rushed in to erase the warmth of those moments as he remembered what the old man had created to destroy any life they would have together.

By the time the other superintendents arrived, Garrett sat with sullen disregard for their congratulations on being one of them now. There was some friendly ribbing and off-colored jokes about his sexual exploits but nothing about the unexpected retirement of the man Garrett replaced. His reputation for rolling with the punches had put a slight strain on Garrett's attitude by the time Big Jim walked into the room and sat his coffee cup on the walnut table.

Their eyes locked as if ready to do combat. The tension between the two men filled the room so that everyone grew silent and pensive. The shuffle of papers in faded file folders made soft sounds against the whistling winds outside. Garrett folded his arms across his chest and leaned back in his leather chair that creaked with his muscular build. He left his folder closed, letting Big Jim know he didn't need to refer to his notes to address any questions that might come up about Bunker operations.

The knowledge that he would need to be more prepared than anyone else was obvious from their past history. Just because Big Jim bought his silence, it didn't mean he would make it easy on him. Garrett knew one mistake could land him in the unemployment line or with a reputation for failure so that no other mining company would hire him. The old man would like nothing better.

"Okay. Let's get started. Welcome, Garrett. Turnbough Lead has every confidence that you'll continue to be the stellar miner we've all come to expect from you." Big Jim stood, imposing his size and power over the group. When Garrett nodded acceptance of the compliment, he continued. "We're on track to meet our tonnage goals this month. However, the grade of the lead is not quite as good as we've seen in recent months."

Charleston began tapping his pencil on his folder. "That's because your new hotshot super over there convinced you the pillar recovery was dangerous. Rocky Fork Mine carries the entire company for high-grade lead, therefore, bringing in the bulk of the revenue."

Big Jim lifted an eyebrow and pooched out his lower lip. "You got anything to say to that, Garrett?"

Garrett swiveled his chair toward Charleston and leaned on the table. "If it takes all the other mines to make it up, then I'd say that's better than losing one man because of sloppy math."

"The only sloppy math is yours. You try so hard to impress Mr. Turnbough that I wouldn't put it past you to juggle the figures to make yourself look like the hero. Then when push comes to shove, you'll start recovering your own pillars down at Bunker with high grade."

"You got it all figured out, don't you, Charleston? If you were a mine engineer, instead of a geologist, you'd know there is a minimum of what can be taken. When you look at those high-grade supports, all you see is dollar signs. I see dead men."

"That's enough," Big Jim growled. "It's my decision, not yours. For now, we'll go with Garrett's suggestions. There's enough money in the coffers to carry us through until the end of the year. If things get tight, we'll make changes. Maybe the markets will rebound a bit. I understand not only China but India is now rushing to increase their purchase of US mineral markets."

"But—" Charleston sounded like a slapped child.

Big Jim held up his hand to stop. "Let's move on. I'm done talking about this."

Charleston clamped his mouth shut as he glared over at Garrett who had turned his attention back to the owner of Turnbough Lead Company. But inside he was both relieved and gratified that the old man had taken his advice. Whatever else Jim was, he loved those mines and the men who made a living getting the lead out for him. Garrett felt confident safety would take preference over money.

The meeting dragged on until lunchtime. Garrett made it underground to visit with the men as they finished their lunch. Shep Abney was now the new mine captain. He was competent and had picked up where Garrett had left off. The men appeared to be in good spirits with their new leadership and felt as though Shep looked out for them when it came to the higher ups. There was some friendly joking about being too good for them now that he was a superintendent of his own mine. Nothing much had changed, including the pillar recovery that Garrett stopped before he left.

Garrett looked at his watch when he stepped off the cage. In just a few hours, the wind had picked up and the sky had turned a dangerous shade of yellow gray. He strode into the main building and stepped inside his old office that now belonged to Shep. A quick call to the Bunker Mine assured him no crisis needed attending. He flipped on the radio and realized they were under a tornado warning. Another call to the mine instructed his people to get ready for power outages. Having the backup generators ready to go to prevent the mine from flooding was paramount. With the yard secured and the colossal trucks that carried the lead to the smelter on standby if the weather worsened, Garrett felt he'd prepared for an emergency. He didn't want boulders of lead rolling on the haul roads if a tornado hit.

As he hung up the phone, he noticed a small yellow receipt from a jewelry store in Farmington. Garrett grinned as he read it. "You dog," he whispered. "You've bought an engagement ring." He replaced the receipt just as he'd found it and exited the office.

He watched Big Jim walking toward his office with Charleston at his side, talking nonstop. Jim kept his head down and nodded periodically. They both saw him at the same time.

"Why aren't you at Bunker?" Charleston stiffened. "Poking around to stir up more trouble?"

Garrett gave him a snide smirk. "Just checking to see if my men had started a coup yet."

Big Jim frowned. "They're not your men anymore, Garrett. Don't be coming around here and making trouble."

Garrett chuckled and slapped Charleston good naturedly on the back. "Just lunch. Didn't think I'd miss this place so much. Used the phone to make sure everything is secure at Bunker. Hear the weather forecast?"

Just then the tornado sirens started. It was an eerie sound, loud and piercing as they walked outside. The thunder sounded like ore being dumped in the mammoth storage containers on the surface of the mines. Clouds looked like dirty blankets sagging with trouble yet to come. People were scrambling for safety as the head frame lowered the cage for the last time until the storm was over.

"We need to go to the basement, Jim." Garrett nudged the man as he stared up at the heavens.

"Hope Nell gets herself to a safe place."

"She will. Now let's go. We'll be needed if that tornado turns our way."

Big Jim nodded and ran after Charleston and Garrett to the safe area under the main building. It had filled quickly. A weather radio was updating every few minutes and someone had brought a computer to follow radar. "It's headed this way," someone moaned. "God help us."

A couple of concerned parents discussed the possibilities. "It was time for those kids to be loading the buses. Think they went back inside?"

Garrett and Jim met each other's eyes, knowing they both thought of Fawn. The idea occurred to Garrett that tornadoes liked two things, mobile homes and schools. Why, he didn't know. Remembering how a F5 tornado had just devastated a school in Oklahoma the year before made him uneasy. Fawn would be responsible for all those little ones. Then he thought of Marcy's son, Joey. The kid was terrified of storms. Should Garrett make a break for it and see if he could help?

The air pressure made everyone's ears pop. Something like the sound of a freight train seemed to be outside. The lights flickered then went out as several gasps broke the silence. Someone opened their cell phone to offer a little light. Garrett retrieved an emergency kit with LED lanterns to dispel the darkness.

Everyone remained standing in place, as if by doing so would lessen the fear taking hold of the room. After all, miners risked their lives every day going underground. But with the EPA and other government watchdogs always snooping around, they possessed a certain level of protection.

Tornadoes were unpredictable. No level of respect or expectation of safety came with Mother Nature's fierce child of destruction.

Thirty minutes passed. The lights flickered again but remained off. The computer showed the storm now barreling toward the next county toward Farmington.

Garrett shoved passed several men and headed up the steps. "I'm out of here." His anxious behavior had Big Jim on his heels. "This can't be good, Jim."

"I'm gonna try and reach Nell. Would you go check on Jeanie Fawn?" There was no confrontational father or god of lead mining now. There was just a man who feared for his family.

Garrett nodded as he pushed open the door at the top of the stairs into daylight. The rest of the building was gone. Nothing but the head frame and smelter remained. He could see the administration building had sustained some damage but remained standing. People started coming out of their hiding places, some looking shell shocked, others with a few scratches.

"You!" Garrett waved to several able-bodied miners as he stumbled over debris. He pointed to different locations. "Start searching for people trapped. Charleston," he yelled, spotting the man walking around in a daze. "Wake up! Make sure all your people are either underground or hunkered down. Make sure the generators kicked in." Stunned, Charleston stared at him. Garrett shook him. "Do your job!"

Charleston swallowed hard and nodded before walking off.

Garrett's truck had been pelted with hail but remained drivable. He continued to give orders as he slid into the front seat of his truck. In seconds, he was racing through the twisted gates and toward the main street in the town of Westfork. Overturned cars, smashed store fronts, and downed trees were the first thing that he spotted. But it was when he turned down the street where the school was located that he slammed on the brakes.

It was gone.

Chapter 12

The kindergarten class grew silent as the sirens roared to life. A few stood up and shivered as tears started down their little faces. Fawn calmly closed the windows and lowered the shades as she began singing a little song the whole class enjoyed. A few sang along while two anxious children raced to her and clung to her legs as if she were a life line. With a pat on the head and a firm hug, Fawn tried to reassure her students. The speaker announced everyone was to move to the hall to take a defensive position in case a tornado actually touched down nearby. Fawn grabbed her attendance leger and ushered everyone into the hallway. Other classes were making haste as they kneeled before lockers and locked their hands over their heads.

She could hear the roar of the storm. This was a bad one. It felt like the building shook as she started to kneel by Marcy Ann's little boy. Frantic he jumped to his feet. "Miss Turnbough! We forgot Ruby Rose! I'll get her." Ruby Rose was the hamster. Joey loved the little rodent. He said he didn't have a dog so Ruby would have to do. "She's 'fraid of storms, Miss Turnbough. Gotta get her."

"Joey! No! Stay here."

Fawn felt him slip away. She dropped her leger and ran after him. Just as she caught up with the little boy the building shook violently. A scream escaped his throat as he turned toward her. The sound of a freight train was the last thing she heard as Fawn pulled Joey into her arms and dived under her desk. She reached out and pulled close a bean bag chair that had been thrown nearby. Then everything went dark.

※

The first sounds Garrett heard were children crying. The building had collapsed on top of them. Somehow, people were pushing debris off and surfacing. He wasn't aware he'd called the mine rescue team until later when someone remarked how calm he'd sounded. Shock would do that to you, he guessed. First responders, miners, parents, and neighbors were on scene almost instantly. Mothers began showing up, screaming their child's name as if by doing so a miracle would appear from the rubble.

The elementary building was a total loss. Twisted metal and beams had actually been a support, keeping most of the children safe as the roof began to disappear or fall in. When the beams fell in, the fallen roof created a low lean-to where the children cowered down on their bellies. The hallway, where many of the children hid, remained standing but everything around it collapsed. Here, too, debris had shoved the children flat while creating a kind of cave of protection. One by one, the children and teachers emerged. Some were bleeding and others helped carry the injured to waiting ambulances.

The grimed-faced principal told Garrett he thought he saw the music teacher being sucked out into the storm. She vanished before his eyes. Tears escaped down his face as he turned to continue the search for others.

"Garrett!" It was Marcy Ann. She'd been working at her salon when the storm hit. "Joey! I can't find him. Garrett, please! Help me find him." Marcy Ann shook violently as she grabbed Garrett's arm.

Garrett patted her back then her cheek. "I will." He tried to sound reassuring. "I need you to stand over there with the other moms so we can work. Can you do that, Marcy?" She nodded as trails of tears brought streaks of mascara down her cheeks. "He was in the back where the worst of it hit. The rescue team is on it. Do you trust me?" Marcy shrugged then nodded. "Good," he said. "We'll work as fast as we can. You can help by keeping calm."

Again the nod as she hugged her abdomen.

Something sour and revolting hit Garrett's stomach as the mine rescue team reached the back of the elementary school where Fawn and Joey would have been. One of the teachers said Fawn had chased the little boy back into the classroom just seconds before the tornado hit. His eyes surveyed the piles of rubble and he wondered if anyone could possibly survive that kind of damage. It looked like a junk pile.

The smell of wet insulation and foreign items blown in to slam on top of the building nearly made Garrett vomit. His heart raced as he frantically moved boards, school supplies, and concrete blocks.

When thunder and lightning again darkened the sky, the mine rescue team dragged Garrett away to a waiting school bus to weather the storm. He shook them off, his temper flaring.

"Get your head in the game, Garrett." Shep shook his friend. "I know Fawn and Joey are in there but you're no good to them if you're killed by lightning." Garrett stared out the door of the bus. Shep nudged him. "Are you listening to me?" Shep was concerned, too. Anytime kids were involved in a tragedy, it was a heart ripped in half. "We'll get 'em."

Garrett's voice took on a hopeless tone. "No one could survive that." He nodded toward the rubble. "Just look at it. A little boy and Fawn." He shook his head as he rubbed his eyes. "She's so fragile and delicate. How could she possibly survive? Tell me that," he whispered. "It'll be dark soon."

"We'll keep looking, Garrett."

"Storm is out of here now!" one of the rescue team members shouted, looking at his computer.

Before anyone could give the "go ahead," Garrett escaped the bus and ran back to where he'd left off in the search. He worked with obsessive motivation to find them, so concentrated on the task at hand, he never realized Big Jim worked alongside him. He saw him lift a bloody child from the rubble. Garrett dropped his work and leaped over several piles of trash to look at the child.

"It's not Joey." Garrett closed his eyes against the possibilities. A paramedic ran up and relieved Jim of the child. "Jim, I appreciate the help but this is getting tricky now. I'd appreciate it if you'd go stand back behind the line with Nell. The other parents may need your confidence about now."

Big Jim looked up at the darkening sky and saw the clouds part, revealing the first star. "If we get through this son, I'm going to have to make a few things right." Garrett shuddered when Big Jim laid a hand on his shoulder. "Nell and I appreciate what you're trying to do here."

Words failed him. In another place and time, Garrett would have loved sparing with the old man. There had never been a time when they hadn't tried to out talk, out insult, and out mine the other. This new Jim rocked Garrett's ability to think straight. The realization that Big Jim believed his daughter dead drove him a little crazy.

Besides the distant rumble of thunder, there were other sounds—women crying, rubble being moved, and voices calling out for loved ones. A tractor started up to pull away some crushed concrete. Men's voices gave instructions as to how to lift, push, or throw away what looked to be immovable objects. The loud click of flood lights turning on made shadows appear as monsters dancing in the night.

The Red Cross had arrived with trucks to serve food but the Baptist church had already opened their recreation building across the street to serve the people who still waited to see their child being raised from the floor of the school. Families of teachers and other staff huddled together as if it were zero degrees on that night in May. The sounds of prayers, a voice singing *Amazing Grace,* swirled on the breezes passing down from the Ozark hills into the town of Westfork. News trucks from St. Louis and Springfield showed up and were already broadcasting in dramatic fashion as the work went on into the night.

Sweat poured from Garrett's body as he feverishly threw debris from where Fawn's room should have been. He stopped to wipe his forehead and looked up at the full moon that seemed to bounce over moving clouds. Then he heard it.

"Stop! Everyone stop! Listen," he demanded with outstretched hands. Then he heard it again, not much more than a whisper.

"Help us."

"Over here! Bring more light! I've found them!"

In seconds, a half dozen men were removing boards as if they performed heart surgery. They didn't want anything else to cave in on whoever called out.

Garrett pointed his flashlight down in a hole and thought he saw a closed hand. He knelt down and touched it. The surprise was when it opened and a little hamster began sniffing the air. He took the rodent and carefully passed it to someone else. "Fawn?" He couldn't see her as he took her hand again. He knew that touch. The memory of asking her whether all rich girls had skin made of silk came to mind. "Fawn. Answer me. Are you hurt?"

"Joey," she coughed. "I think…" Then her voice faded.

"Everybody knows what to do. Are you ready?"

Garrett didn't have to look to see determination in his team. They wouldn't let him down. When the last board was removed, they saw Fawn with her legs drawn up, cradling the little boy against her chest. Blood covered the side of her face and down Joey's back. Her eyes flickered open as large hands removed the little boy from her protection. Garrett handed him off then turned back to Fawn. He knelt down again and shined the flashlight all over her body. Shep moved in. He was their first-aid man and had trained as a paramedic for the volunteer fire department.

"Fawn, I need to ask you a few questions before I get you out. Okay?" Shep's voice sounded confident.

She tried to nod her head but cringed as more blood began to seep out of her shoulder.

Shep turned to Garrett who began to frown. "I see it. Her shoulder has been punctured. She'll bleed to death if we don't get her out of here soon. Let's move. Nice and slow men. Is that helicopter on its way?" Shep called out. He was reassured it was almost here. It would land at the airstrip outside of town. That was the only place that didn't have some kind of debris covering it. "Garrett, she's going to be fine. We need to get a cuff on her neck."

Fawn held onto Garrett's hand. Taken aback at how strong her grip felt, Garrett wanted to believe she would survive.

"Don't leave me," she moaned.

"Never. Who would I have to make me crazy?"

This made her smile as she closed her eyes. "I'm sorry."

"We'll talk about that later. I need you to be really strong, Fawn, and do what Shep tells you."

"Okay," she whispered. "Garrett, I have to tell you something." She took a deep breath and licked her dry cracked lips.

Shep pushed him aside as he slipped the collar around Fawn's neck. "Fawn, we're ready to lift you out. It's probably going to hurt."

Fawn opened her eyes and searched for Garrett. He kneeled down beside her and smiled. "I'll be at the hospital. Promise. Your folks are waiting over there. I'm surprised your momma isn't here telling Shep how to do his job." Garrett faked a chuckle but Fawn let out a scream as they lifted her onto the stretcher. He thought his heart would leap out of his chest at the sound. "Careful!" he demanded.

"Stay out of the way, Garrett," Shep ordered. "I know what I'm doin'. She's hurt bad. I'll fly to the hospital with her and Joey. You take Marcy Ann."

Garrett wasn't used to taking orders from his best friend. But, this once, he had no choice. Fawn cried out again as they lifted her onto the stretcher. She fainted just as her eyes met his. Grabbing her hand, Garrett ran alongside the gurney to the ambulance that would take her to the airstrip. Her parents waited impatiently as they lifted her inside. Nell's tears were a mixture of relief and fear as she saw the chunk of wood protruding from Fawn's shoulder. Big Jim held onto his wife, pretending to offer support when in fact he needed her small frame to keep his knees from buckling underneath him.

Garrett raced to the airstrip where Marcy Ann stood watching her little boy being loaded onto the helicopter. She was beside herself with relief but knew her son was badly injured nonetheless. Garrett guided her to his truck and had to physically fasten her into her seatbelt. Speed limits meant nothing as they raced through the countryside to Farmington. The hospital was nearly an hour away on a good day. The tornado had spun itself out and, besides flooding along the Huzzah River, there wasn't much to be concerned about that would prevent them from reaching the hospital.

Garrett wondered how Fawn's parents would get to the hospital but imagined Jim would get a police escort if he asked. Everyone connected to Westfork owed some kind of allegiance to Turnbough Lead. You didn't screw with the boss putting bread and butter on the table. They would be fine. At Garrett's request, Marcy Ann called his parents to let him know about Joey and Fawn. He knew neither hell nor high water would stop them from coming. Shep would be on the helicopter and could fill him in when they arrived.

He tried to ignore the constant crying coming from Marcy Ann. Thanks to Fawn, Joey would probably be fine. He wasn't so sure of Fawn's condition. She looked like death warmed over in his opinion. After parking, both bolted to the emergency room where other parents waited for the results of their children's examinations. Some had suffered less serious injuries but needed medical attention. Directed to the second floor waiting area, Garrett and Marcy entered with trepidation.

"Why here?" Marcy gasped for breath. Keeping up with Garrett had been a struggle.

"This is the surgery wing," Garrett said, looking around for someone to give him more information. He spotted Shep coming through doors that whooshed open. "Shep. How are they?"

Marcy fell into Shep's arms and hugged him. "Thank you for going with Joey."

Shep rubbed her back. "He's quite a little trooper. He has a knot on his head and some nasty cuts and bruises. They're prepping him for surgery."

"Why? What's wrong?" The panic returned to her voice.

Shep pushed her at arm's length. "His leg is a mess. It's broken in several places. I need to take you back to fill out some paper work. I did what I could but I didn't know whether he was allergic to anything. Come on." He led her toward the double doors. "Garrett, I'll be back in a second."

True to his word, Shep returned and faced Garrett who had started to pace. "Fawn is not so good."

"I want to see her," Garrett demanded.

"That's not up to me. She needs surgery too."

"What's wrong with her, Shep?" Garrett ran his fingers through his hair. His clothes were damp and dirty. He smelled of perspiration and garbage. "She's not going to die, though, right?"

Shep started to speak when Big Jim and Nell entered the waiting room. Big Jim fired question after question at Shep until he sighed and took them back to the surgery center desk. He returned moments later to find Garrett pacing again.

"I should be back there," he snapped. "I love her. Take me."

Shep was used to Garrett's demanding ways and usually rolled with the punches. This time he couldn't. "You're not family, Garrett."

"Like hell," Garrett roared. "She's been at my side since she was—" He choked.

Shep laid a hand on his shoulder but Garrett knocked it off.

"Let me see what I can do. But if Big Jim says 'no' then it's 'no.'"

Garrett nodded as he tried to square his shoulders. He swallowed hard and wiped his face of emotion. Shep soon stood in the double doors and motioned for him to come back. The waiting area had a curtain, partially drawn, as Nell and Big Jim stood just outside it.

"Oh, Garrett." Nell fell into his arms and didn't appear to mind that he looked like a gutter rat at the moment. "You found her. Thank you." She reached up and kissed him on his cheek. "And little Joey, how is he?" Nell could see Marcy at the end of the hall talking to the doctor.

"I think his leg is in pretty bad shape but it's not life threatening. What does the doctor say about Fawn?" Garrett couldn't see her with so many people working on her. Big Jim filled up the one area not blocked by medical staff. He reminded Garrett of a mighty oak that was about to topple. "Jim?" Garrett reached out and touched the man's arm.

"Huh? Oh, Garrett. You're here." Jim stuck out his hand and grabbed Garrett's when he didn't respond fast enough. "You saved my girl."

It wasn't a thank you but Garrett knew that's what he meant. "What did the doctor say, Jim?"

"Broken arm, some internal bleeding, and that stake-of-a-thing has to be removed from her shoulder. They're not sure what they'll find when they go in. He said..." Jim turned his eyes on Garrett and stared at him with contempt.

"Said what?" Garrett couldn't help but sound anxious.

Jim turned back to stare at the figure in the bed. "She'll pull through. She's my daughter, by God."

Nell slipped her hand around Garrett's arm. "He's just worried, Garrett. We all are. I'm so glad you're here."

The medical team started to move Fawn's bed out of her tiny waiting room toward what would be several hours of surgery. Garrett caught his breath as he looked at her.

He stood on one side and walked along while her parents took up the vigil on the other side. Big Jim caught hold of the bed and stopped it. He reached over and tenderly touched Fawn's hair.

"You hang in there, girl. You hear me. Don't make

your momma cry." His voice, even now sounded demanding.

Her eyes fluttered open as she nodded obediently. She turned her head toward Garrett and smiled then cringed. "Garrett," she whispered.

He reached over and kissed her bruised cheek. "Listen to your dad, Jeanie Fawn. We need you." His eyes cut to Big Jim then back to Fawn. "I need you."

"Mr. Turnbough, we've got to go." It was the nurse.

Both men withdrew their hands from the bed railings. Nell started a quiet cry into a tissue as the sounds of machines beeping and quiet voices floated down the hall.

Chapter 13

Morning light spilled through the windows of the room where Garrett waited with Big Jim and Nell. His parents had come, as he knew they would. He knew they were concerned for Fawn but wanted to encourage Marcy Ann as well. They loved the little boy, in spite of the breakup. They waited until Fawn was out of surgery before leaving. The surgeon said her injuries, although serious, were no longer life threatening. Her shoulder was of some concern. They wouldn't know for a while if she'd have full use of that shoulder and arm. More surgery might be needed down the road.

Marcy Ann was allowed to sleep in the child's room. She was comforted, knowing he would be good as knew after some physical therapy. Little boys healed quickly and Joey was pretty tough. Garrett had gone to see him after he'd come out of recovery. He stood with Shep, listening to the surgeon talk to Marcy outside Joey's room. While Shep began a litany of comforting words to Marcy, Garrett stepped inside Joey's room to have a look. His once-little leg appeared huge wrapped in so much protection. It no longer looked like it belonged to a five year old.

When he laid his hand on the boy's head, Marcy came to the other side of the bed. "He looks so helpless." Garrett touched his pale cheek. "Marcy, are you all right?"

She cut her eyes sharply up at him and frowned. "Yes." She exhaled loudly. "Thank you for finding him. You saved his life."

Garrett shook his head. "No. Fawn did that." He related how he'd found them under a smashed desk, Fawn clinging to him tight against her chest.

Pain flooded her eyes as she looked back at her son. "You should go. I'll be fine. Shep said he'd sit with me a while."

Garrett nodded before leaning over and kissing the little boy on the forehead. "Okay. I'll come back in a while to check on you. Let me know if you need anything." He watched her pull up a chair close to the bed. She never looked at him again.

That had been hours ago. Garrett stretched as he stood then glanced at his watch. The smell of coffee filled the room. He wanted a shower. In the washroom, he made an effort to remove some of the grime and smell that clung to his body and clothes. Maybe he'd get to go in and see Fawn before heading back to the lead belt where mining continued, in spite of hell and high water.

Big Jim stood at the coffee machine when Garrett reappeared. Nell was just waking up and smiled at Garrett as he brought her a cup of coffee. She blew on it, very much the way Fawn did when she drank hot tea. Big Jim disappeared for a few minutes then came back for Nell.

"She's awake, Nell. The nurse says she can have one visitor at a time."

Nell stood slowly and looked down at Garrett who had eased down on the couch next to her. "You go in, honey. I know you've got to get back to work. You'll probably be just the right medicine she needs."

Big Jim stepped in Garrett's path as he sat his own cup of coffee down on the counter. "I don't think that's a good idea."

Garrett stepped around him. "I knew you'd turn back into being a jerk, Jim. I just didn't think it would be so soon."

Big Jim reached out and grabbed his arm. "Don't be a smart ass. I just don't want you to go in there and start confessing things she can't handle right now." His warning came low enough where Nell couldn't hear him.

Garrett jerked free of his hold and leaned in to speak into his ear. "You, of all people, shouldn't be telling me how to treat Fawn, old man. Besides, I don't have anything to confess. You do."

Fawn remained on the surgical floor where staff could keep a close eye on her. The nurse, exiting from her room, announced she'd probably be moved to a regular room by day's end. She smiled flirtatiously at Garrett but he failed to notice as he hurried to Fawn's bedside.

She appeared to sleep as he reached down and lifted her hand in his. She sighed as her eyes fluttered open to gaze at Garrett's smiling face.

"You gave me a scare, Fawn," he whispered as he squeezed her hand.

"Joey?" For a second, a look of panic made her forehead crease and her eyes narrow.

Garrett leaned over and pushed a few strands of hair away from her delicate face. "Good. He's going to be fine, thanks to you."

"Have you been here long?" She licked her lips and Garrett immediately got her a drink of water.

Garrett smiled down at her. "All night. Mom and Dad came too. Your folks are in the waiting room. Nell let me come first since I probably have to head back to the mine. Your dad isn't going to want his newest mine superintendent to miss work."

Another bewildered look crossed her face. "Superintendent? When did that happen?" She cleared her throat and motioned for another drink.

Garrett cocked his head. "Don't you remember the

other day at the post office? You told me congratulations?" He chuckled and took her hand again. "Guess you got hit on that hard head of yours too."

"I didn't know, Garrett." Fawn shook her head as it dawned on her they were talking about two different things that day. "Dad never told me."

Garrett felt confused as the smile disappeared from his face. "Then what were you talking about?"

"My turn, Garrett." Nell came alongside of the bed and patted her daughter on the good arm. "How's my girl? You are looking just fine this morning."

Garrett stepped back and kissed Nell on the cheek. "I've got to go." He looked back down at Fawn. "I'll be back tomorrow to see you."

She offered a weak smile and nodded. "Thanks for rescuing me, Garrett."

Nell hugged him one last time and walked him to the door. "I'll call you later and let you know how she's doing, sweetheart. Don't you worry. Big Jim will make sure she is well taken care of."

Garrett pushed through the double doors to leave the surgical section only to see Big Jim leaning against a wall, checking his cell phone. He seemed awkward with the device. "Damn phone. Why does everything have to be so complicated these days?"

Garrett started past him "You tell me."

Big Jim followed. Garrett planned to take the stairs so the old man would stop. But he didn't. "Hold on."

"I've got to get to work."

"I want you to promise me you'll not say anything to Fawn until I have a chance to speak with her first."

Garrett had practically run down a flight of stairs when he stopped short. He turned around and frowned. "And when will that be? Did you even tell her I got a promotion?"

Big Jim raised an eyebrow in irritation. "I've been a little busy. When I am with Fawn, I don't usually care to talk about you. Promise me."

Garrett turned and continued down the stairs. "I've made my last promise to you," he called back. "When I come back to see her, I'm telling her the truth. Fire me if you want."

❧❧❧

The tornado hit Westfork hard. Like most severe storms, it chose random targets to destroy. The main building where Garrett and others had waited out the storm now looked like it had imploded on one end. The head frame thirty feet away looked as if it had never been touched. Several stores on the square now resembled rubble piles. Across the street the shops were untouched and open for business. Trees blocked the haul road so that the colossal ore trucks became towing machines to clear the way.

If the mines couldn't get the ore to the mill, then

there wasn't much point in having hundreds of men go underground.

Cleanup was in full swing when Garrett passed through town. He stopped at the firehouse to get news of casualties or missing persons. The police found the music teacher one hundred yards from the school. It surprised everyone that she had been the only fatality. Most of the children suffered only cuts and bruises.

The more serious injuries had been taken to either the Salem or Farmington hospitals. Most had been treated and released the following morning. Only Joey, along with two little girls, sustained wounds or broken bones that required surgery. Of those three, Joey had been the most severe.

It wasn't difficult to see the path of the storm as Garrett drove toward the Bunker mine. Large swaths of trees across the rolling hills had been twisted into pretzel shapes with their bark stripped clean. He dodged a few limbs across the road and stopped to help an old man right his mailbox that had been blown sideways by the wind.

News reached him the night before that all was well at his mine. Other than the power being off for a few hours, very little had changed from the morning before. The yard showed activity as Garrett parked his truck then made his way toward his office. Out of respect, several men stopped him to inquire about Big Jim's daughter. The safety manager informed Garrett he'd met with the men earlier to emphasize how important it was to make sure they had a safe place at home in case of storms. Garrett thanked him for attending to the business of getting the lead out. He made it underground to speak to the men and insisted those who had injured children take the rest of the day off to attend to their families. Some of his people had been out all night helping others. That made for a dangerous combination when working with mining equipment, explosives, and boulders the size of a tank.

He ordered lunch and twenty pies from the Bixby Café and General Store for the day shift since the shops had not suffered any damage. The gesture was repeated for the night shift and more pies for third shift. The cost came out of his own pocket. Knowing a miner's mentality, Garrett knew the men would be putting the welfare of the mine first. That's just the way hard rock miners rolled.

Their wives, sweethearts, and families knew this was the way of life they'd chosen. Nowhere else could a man with just a high school education make twenty dollars an hour. Most of them made more than the school teachers with master's degrees. But their loyalty to Turnbough Lead would not be compromised. So he told the mine captains to go easy on the men and make sure they took plenty of breaks. He didn't want any accidents due to fatigue.

It was nearly seven before Garrett made his way back to Westfork. He desperately wanted to go to bed but when he heard at the gas station several churches were continuing with the cleanup around the school, Garrett went to help. At ten he went home to his apartment, listening to a message from his mother concerned about Fawn and Joey. The second one had also been his mother saying she'd gotten the information from Nell. He'd taken a shower at the mine earlier in the day but needed another one after helping the Baptists and Methodists with cleanup.

He sat down on the couch and wondered about Fawn's horses and the black cat that followed her everywhere. A fog descended on him as he made a mental list to go out the next morning before work and check on them for her. She loved her animals. As his eyes grew heavy, Garrett wondered if she'd ever love him like she once did so long ago. He knew he should move to the bed but the darkness of exhaustion shoved him into a deep sleep.

Chapter 14

Fawn listened to the doctor insist she take it easy for the next few weeks. He consulted earlier with the surgeon and was able to convince her the baby was in no danger. The relief that washed over her forced a flood of tears. With gentle reassurance, the doctor patted her good shoulder and suggested she stay with someone, maybe her mother, since she had no one at home to take care of her. There was no reason why the baby couldn't be carried to term. Fawn made it clear she'd not told her family about the baby and would appreciate him keeping the secret just a little longer.

"I've left more instructions with your nurse, Fawn. I'll see you in a couple of weeks. If there is any change or Nervous Nellie concerns just call me. You can come right in." He shoved his hands into his pockets and smiled a big grin. "Any questions?"

Fawn confessed her fears through multiple questions, some being asked more than once in a different way. When the doctor started to laugh, she smiled and exhaled. "Okay. I feel better."

"I see no reason why you can't go home tomorrow. Your surgeon wants you out of this place. The hospital is not a very good place to escape germs. I don't want you getting an infection."

"Let me go today. I want to see my students."

"Now you listen to me, young lady. You're not to be going to school. Besides, I don't believe there's a building for you to go to. Seeing all of that will not, let me repeat, will not be good for you or the baby. Understood?"

Fawn frowned, thinking of all her little children and of how concerned they must be. "Understood, Doctor. Thank you."

After the doctor left, breakfast arrived. She pushed the eggs around with her fork but managed to eat her toast and sip the hot tea. Deep in thought about the storm, Fawn didn't notice Marcy Ann enter the room.

"Fawn?"

The voice sounded so timid Fawn was taken aback. "Marcy Ann." She offered a nervous smile and pushed the tray away. "How's our little guy?"

Marcy inched closer. "Starting to complain so I guess he's on the mend."

A stretch of silence welled up between the two women. "I hear his leg needed two surgeries," Fawn said.

Marcy nodded and moved to the side of the bed. She rested both hands on the railing at the head of the bed. She started telling Fawn about the shape of his leg and what the doctor's prognosis was for Joey. "He's not going to be happy about staying out of the creek and riding his bike."

Fawn laughed. "No. But I'd really like for him to take care of our little hamster, Ruby Rose for the summer. I'll buy all the supplies and food. I'll be staying with my folks for a while and I know my mother will never let a rodent in her house. I could even pay him as if it were a job. He loves that thing. My dad said someone at the fire station is keeping it until they hear what to do with it."

Marcy's soft laugh surprised Fawn. "Well, I can't say I like them either but right now I'd grab the moon for Joey if he wanted it."

Fawn smiled and another crevice of silence followed.

Marcy took a deep breath and squeezed the bars on the railing. "So how are you, Fawn?" She cleared her throat. "I hope you're okay."

Fawn caught the hidden meaning. She didn't know whether to order her out or see where the line of questioning was headed. "My shoulder will heal. I'll need some physical therapy and I'm probably going to be able to predict the weather for the next fifty years."

Both women forced a nervous laugh.

Marcy patted the railing before turning to leave. "Well, I better go check on Joey."

"Thanks for coming."

Fawn watched Marcy Ann turn back and tenderly put a kiss on the side of her head. "Thank you for saving my boy, Fawn." Tears pooled at the corners of her eyes.

"I'm kind of fond of the little rascal." Fawn used her good arm to touch Marcy's face. "Don't let him see you cry."

Marcy nodded and tried to compose herself. "I'm just going to come right out and ask, Fawn. Is the baby okay."

"Yes. I just talked to the doctor." Fawn watched Marcy smile again. This time it appeared genuine. "You are the only person who knows about the baby. Thank you for keeping my secret."

Marcy rubbed her arms as if she'd gotten a chill. "I'm glad, Fawn. Your secret is safe with me for as long as you want."

"That might be for a very long time. I'm planning on leaving Westfork as soon as I'm up and about. Both of us need a break and a little breathing room. I have the means to start over so I think it's best if I move on."

"I—I don't know what to s—say," Marcy stuttered.

"You deserve a better life. I'm a constant reminder of failure both to Garrett and my father. I've always been like a ping pong ball between them. Both of them care more about winning than they do about my feelings. I wanted to come back to Westfork and I feel like I belonged. But I just got caught up in another tug-of-war between two hard headed men. I don't want that for my child."

"Westfork is your home," Marcy said with hesitation. "It doesn't seem fair."

Fawn sighed. "I'll start over. Kathleena wants me to move to Oklahoma where she and her husband live. I won't be so far away that my folks can't come for a visit and vice versa. She may be Garret's sister but she always takes my side. She also won't ask too many questions."

"You two were always inseparable." Marcy walked to the door. "Will you come by to see Joey before you leave?"

Fawn promised to drop by later in the day when her mother could help her. "You tell him I better see a happy face. Be sure to tell him about Ruby Rose."

Although she smiled, Fawn noted a great sadness weighing on the woman. They shared a common problem; the father of their unborn children was the notorious Garrett Horton.

೭⊃೭⊃

Fawn surveyed the town of Westfork as her mother drove her home the next morning. Even though she knew of the destruction, seeing it took her breath away. She covered her mouth several times to keep from crying out in agony. Insisting that she be taken to the school met with some resistance from Nell but Fawn won out in the end. Even though the weather was one of those days the Chamber of Commerce dreamed about putting in their tourist brochures the gloom of destruction cast an eerie cloud over the scene.

"I want to get out, Mom."

Their car stopped in the cleared parking lot.

"Wait until I come around to help you out, Fawn." Even as Nell raced around the front of the car, her daughter was already opening the door.

"I'm fine, Mom. You're hovering and it's making me crazy." Fawn tried to sound appreciative and amused but in truth she wanted her mother to relax. She leaned against the front of the car, feeling its warmth seep into her back. For some reason, she felt cold as her eyes took in the scene before her. The touch of her mother's hand slipping around her arm gave Fawn strength to stand up straight.

"How did Joey and I survive this?"

"Only the good Lord knows, Jeanie Fawn. But I am so thankful you did. You've been given a second chance, darling. It's up to you to find out why. Make it count." Nell watched the bulldozers scooping up what once was a school and then dump the debris into dump trucks. The sounds were deafening. "I think we should head home."

Fawn nodded and took small tired steps back to get in the car. What if she had lost the baby? As her mother started the car, Fawn laid a hand on her stomach and smiled. Together they would start over and be happy. Her mother would not like her moving to Oklahoma where she couldn't see the baby every day. But after Fawn told her everything about Garrett she would understand. But as of right now Garrett walked on water as far as Nell was concerned.

"Are you feeling okay, honey. You have been so quiet. I'm just concerned." Nell pulled into the driveway and tapped the horn. The couple who worked on site rushed out, waving to Fawn. They were in their fifties now. Sid kept the grounds and maintained the equipment while his wife Rosie made sure the inside of the mansion remained a showcase.

"Yes. I'm fine."

Sid opened her door. "Fawn. Oh my goodness you look pretty as a wildflower."

Fawn smiled and slid out. The couple, never having children of their own, enjoyed fussing over Fawn. Rosie clapped her hands together like a small child. "Come inside now. I made your favorite soup and a big apple crisp for dessert."

Nell hooked her arm through Fawn's and followed the couple into the back door. Greeted by the smells of homemade vegetable soup mixed with cooking apples made Fawn feel at peace. She wanted to forget the prospect of what lay ahead of her. Today, she'd pretend all was right with the world.

Nell sat down at the table as Rosie filled two bowls with the steaming soup and sat it before each woman. "Did you ever call Garrett back, Fawn? He called a half a dozen times while I was there. Are you angry because he didn't come to visit? You know he was filling in for several men who lost their homes during the storm."

Fawn took a spoon full and blew across it before sipping. "No. Every time I thought of it someone dropped by to visit then I'd fall asleep."

Nell clucked. "Well, that's a relief."

She eyed her cautiously. "Why is that, Mom?"

"I like that boy. I don't know what broke the two of you up years ago but clearly he is still smitten with you. Why the poor boy nearly came unglued the other night when he waited for you to come out of surgery. With all that pacing, I thought for sure the hospital would have to replace the carpet by the time they told us you'd be fine." Nell laughed. "I'm telling you that boy had tears in his eyes."

Fawn paused with her spoon midair. "Probably thought I'd die and he'd lose his chance to marry the mines."

Her snarky tone made Nell point an angry finger at her. "That'll be enough of that talk, young lady. You won't be bad mouthing that good man in this house. He saved your life and because of that, I still have my daughter. I'll never forget that."

Fawn put her spoon down. "Sorry, Mom. I know

Garrett better than you do. He comes across all sweet and respectful with you but he makes no bones about wanting to run Turnbough Lead. He thinks the only way to do that is through me. That's why I didn't call him. He would have seen it as a sign I was falling for all that country boy charm he spreads around."

Nell leaned back in her chair and grinned. "He is a charmer. Why if I was thirty years younger…"

"Mother. Really?" Fawn had to laugh. "Even you are under his spell."

"If the truth be told you are too. You are just afraid to admit it."

Fawn finished off her soup and nodded at Rosie when she held up a piece of warm apple crisp pie with ice cream. "I'd rather think about this pie right now, Mom. Rosie, I love you for doing this."

Rosie patted Fawn's hair and turned back to cleaning up the kitchen.

"What if he comes by? He'll probably call today and find out you've been released."

"Unavailable."

Nell began clearing the table. "You are as stubborn as your daddy."

Fawn frowned at the thought of being like her father. He was indeed stubborn but he was also cruel, manipulative, and a severe task master. While she was growing up, he rarely praised her for good grades or singing a solo at church. However, if her grade in trigonometry or Chemistry slipped to a B+, she had to meet with him in the study for a little chat. There would be tears and promises to do better next time. It wasn't until the accident that she saw something vulnerable in his eyes and a quiver in his voice that made her aware how much he loved her. What kind of disappointment would result when she told him Garrett was the father of his first grandchild?

⁂

"She was released? When?"

Garrett had made the hour drive to Farmington Hospital without calling first. Fawn never returned his calls. He wasn't sure if her father was intercepting them or she just wasn't up to making calls. Either way, he'd not seen her for several days. The thought of seeing her again drove him to get his work completed in record time so he could take off early. Problems at the mine delayed him until it was after six by the time he got on the road. The days were longer now so driving on the winding roads made the trip less stressful. There was still plenty of daylight by the time he reached the hospital.

The nurse looked at her computer. "Looks like this morning."

Garrett tapped the counter with his fingertips and turned toward the hall where Marcy Ann's little boy would be. He'd stopped at the gift shop downstairs and bought him a remote control helicopter. They had gladly stuck it in a gift bag with superheroes on it and added some tissue paper.

He found the room easy enough and was surprised to see Shep Abney reading a story to the boy. As soon as Joey saw him, he grew excited and waved.

"Garrett, come see what Shep brought me."

Shep stood and let Garrett come in closer. "What you got there, little buddy?"

Joey showed him several books on taking care of hamsters. There was a couple of picture books that looked like there was going to be a funny story involved. "Miss Turnbough needs me to take care of Ruby Rose this summer. She is buying all the stuff to do it."

He was talking so fast Garrett had to laugh. "Well, she's a pretty good teacher to let you do that. She must really trust you."

Nodding, with a big grin, Joey showed his missing top two teeth. "She does. Shep knows all about animals. He said he could help me change that stuff in the bottom of the cage when I needed to do it because Mommy said she wasn't going to do it."

Garrett turned to look at Shep and cocked his head in confusion. Both men locked stares. "I guess Shep is a pretty good guy then." Shep looked at him with a new kind of challenge. He'd heard it in his voice the night of the storm. Now he saw it in his friend's eyes. "I bet he can help you with this, too." Garrett handed the gift bag to him and waited for the cheer of appreciation.

"Thanks, Garrett."

A feminine voice entered the room. "Thanks for what?" It was Marcy Anne, carrying two sacks from a local fast food restaurant. Her eyes went to Garrett then to Shep who had gone rigid.

"Just brought Joey something to occupy his time when he goes home. Looks like Shep," Garrett cut his eyes to his best friend, "beat me to it. When does he get to go home, Marcy?"

Marcy sat the burger bags on the moveable cart and took out a cheese burger and fries for her son.

She smiled at Joey and ruffled his hair only to have him pull away in embarrassment. "The doctor said maybe in a couple of days."

"If you need anything Marcy—"

"I'll take care of it, Garrett," Shep interrupted. He nodded his head toward the hall. "We need to talk. Marcy, I want you there too."

Garrett walked into the hall and put his hands on his hips as he took up a defensive stance. His eyes went from Marcy, who suddenly had a blush on her face, to Shep who looked grim faced. "What is it, Shep?"

"Marcy and I got married a week ago." Shep swallowed loudly as if he were losing his nerve. "We eloped and went to a justice of the peace in Salem."

Garrett's eyes searched Shep's face as his hands dropped to his side. "Is this a joke?"

Shep raised his chin as if by doing so he would be

taller than Garrett. "No. I love Marcy Ann. I always have, even in school I had a crush on her."

A grin spread across Garrett's mouth as he stuck out his hand. "Congratulations, you old dog." Garrett pumped his best friend's hand, more relieved than Shep would ever know. "Why didn't you tell me?"

Shep looked down at Marcy who had gone pale. "Marcy."

Garrett looked suspiciously at his former girlfriend. "What?"

"I'm pregnant," Marcy blurted out.

Garrett staggered back a step, remembering the night she'd showed up at his apartment. "Pregnant?"

"Don't worry," she snapped. "It's not yours." She looked up at Shep. "One night I saw Shep and we started talking and—"

"One thing led to another and I'm going to be a father." There was a hint of pride in Shep's voice. "You clearly were no longer interested and I'm afraid I took advantage of the situation and made my move."

Marcy slipped an arm around Shep's waist. "I'm not so sure who took advantage of who but we're going to make this work."

Garrett slapped Shep on the arm. "I knew you were seeing someone. I understand your hesitation to tell me. I'm sorry I made both of you so miserable. Seems like I've been doing that a lot lately."

"Which brings us to another matter, Garrett?" Shep sighed as he looked down at Marcy then at his friend. "There's something you need to know about Fawn."

Chapter 15

"Pregnant? Fawn's pregnant?" Garrett choked on his own words.

Shep led him to a nearby empty waiting room. "I don't have to ask if the baby is yours."

Garrett sat down on the edge of a couch. He ran his fingers through his thick, sandy-colored hair then across his face as if removing cobwebs. "Why didn't she tell me?"

Shep looked at Marcy with anger for the first time as she cleared her throat.

"I may have implied I was pregnant with your child."

Garrett jumped up. "What?"

Shep growled. "Sit down and listen for once."

Marcy explained how she'd run into Fawn at the

doctor's and the little scene at the pharmacy counter. "She was already in her car when Shep pulled up to get me in your truck. I'm sure she thought it was you and I never told her any different." Marcy looked to Shep for support but was once again reminded she'd hurt him too by deceiving Fawn. "I wanted to hurt her. I blamed her for breaking us up." She laid her hand on Shep's leg and squeezed. "I realize now we were no good for each other. I thought I wanted you but I was just reaching for something that would never make me happy."

Garrett drove faster than he should have over the twisting roads that led back to Westfork. When he realized his speed, he would take his foot off the accelerator to try and refocus on the bombshell just dropped on him. His thoughts rambled from Shep marrying Marcy to Joey at last being a part of a real family. Then he went to a dark place to drag up the image of Jim Turnbough followed by Fawn being buried alive in rubble where she could have died.

He pulled his truck into the Bixby Café parking lot and let his truck idle. He needed to calm down before he confronted Fawn and her father. He lowered his window and turned off the engine to breathe in the evening air. It was almost nine o'clock. There was still some daylight this time of year. He knew the sound of whippoorwills would soon fill the night with their repetitive songs. How many times had he sat on his mom's front porch and counted the whippoorwill sounds with Fawn? She loved those night creatures, even when they were so noisy you couldn't sleep.

His thoughts turned back to Shep. "Fawn's under the assumption only her doctors and Marcy Ann know she's pregnant. But I overheard the surgeon express some concern to Jim before he operated on her. Nell was with Fawn so she is clueless."

Garrett started the engine and pulled out onto the highway that led to Pucky Huddle Drive where the Turnbough Mansion stood looking down on the lead mining kingdom it had created.

By the time he pulled into the driveway, the solar lights throughout the landscaping were trying to flicker on for the night.

He hadn't meant to bang so hard on the door or ring the doorbell so many times. When Nell opened the door, she smiled then gasped as he pushed in without an invitation.

"Where's Fawn?"

Nell looked a little concerned. "Resting. I'm not sure this is a good time to visit, Garrett. Maybe if you had come earlier."

Big Jim walked into the foyer with his hands shoved in his jean pockets. "What's the problem?" he stormed.

"Nell, I'm sorry to barge in but earlier I was at the hospital looking for Fawn."

"Oh dear. Jim, didn't you call him like I said?" Nell put one hand on her hip in disgust before looking back at

Garrett. "I'm so sorry, honey. Let me see if she is still up."

Nell disappeared up the spiral staircase that looked like something out of *Gone With the Wind*.

The two men glared at each other until Big Jim finally looked at his watch. "Come back another time."

"No," Garrett growled.

"You have an early day tomorrow. MSHA is doing an inspection."

"No," Garrett repeated. He knew the Mine Safety and Health Administration didn't like to be kept waiting or given excuses, but he really didn't think that was as important as clearing up a few things concerning Big Jim's daughter.

Jim walked to the massive front doors and opened one. "Leave or I'm calling the police."

"No." Garrett walked over to the door and slammed it shut. "Let's just clear the air right now. You have no intention of ever telling Fawn about how you set me up three weeks before our wedding so someone could take those photos. I would never have cheated on her. But pictures don't lie, do they?" Garrett was inches from Big Jim's face. The old man snarled but didn't flinch. "You realized I really did love your daughter and you just couldn't stand a country boy like me being part of your life. I wasn't good enough. You knew I came from humble beginnings and was a hard worker. But that didn't matter. You wanted some Harvard grad or fancy lawyer from St. Louis to marry Fawn. I didn't have a pedigree."

"That's enough," Big Jim barked.

"You destroyed any trust Fawn had in me. You made her unable to trust any man ever again. You didn't just wreck my life you crushed the very soul out of your only child."

"Is that true, Daddy?" It was the small, horrified voice of Fawn who stood at the bottom of the stairs with her mother's arm around her waist. "Daddy, did you manipulate Garrett into appearing like he was sleeping around on me?"

Nell's face had grown cold and contorted. "Answer her, Jim," she demanded.

"I thought I was doing the right thing, Fawn." He didn't apologize. "I still think I'm right. He wanted the mines not you."

Fawn took a step toward her father. Her eyes shifted to Garrett. It was as if the blinders fell from her eyes. "Garrett," she whispered in agony. "What have I done to you?"

Garrett nudged past the old man and caught Fawn in his arms, careful not to hurt her shoulder. He turned back to her father. "You can keep your mines, old man. Nothing is worth losing her again. Find another superintendent because I quit. You aren't the only mining operation in this country."

Fawn leaned into Garrett and felt him pull her into the living room. "Nell, I want to talk to Fawn alone."

Nell pointed at her husband to head for the kitchen. He obeyed by stomping from the foyer.

"Marcy Ann told me everything." Garrett pulled Fawn down on the sofa and ran his hand down the back of her hair. She had not dressed for bed yet. Her long legs looked slender and firm barely covered by her jean cut-offs.

The shirt sported the school logo where she had worked.

"I don't see how that changes anything, Garrett. You're going to be a father twice." Her voice quaked with uncertainty.

Garrett smiled, no longer able to resist kissing her trembling lips. "That baby is Shep's, not mine. Marcy only pretended in order to make you jealous. After you saved Joey, she had to fess-up. Besides she is now married to Shep."

A quiet laugh escaped her mouth as the tears rolled down the side of her face.

"I love you, Fawn. I always have. Will you marry me?"

"I've made your life miserable. Why on earth would you want me back?"

"Because loving, fighting, and living with you is the best life I could possibly ask for."

Fawn started nodding as a smile spread across her lips. "Yes. How soon do you want me to start making you second guess your decision to marry me?"

"This Sunday. We've got time to get the marriage license and we'll have the preacher do it right after morning services."

Fawn laughed. "You're crazy."

Garrett pulled her into his arms and captured her mouth with his. "Leave with me tonight. I don't want to take the chance on Jim talking you out of it."

"I may never speak to him again. I doubt he'll try and talk me out of it. I bet my mother is in there right now, giving him a severe tongue lashing."

"I need to know how you—"

Fawn laid her finger on his wide mouth and stroked his bottom lip. "I love you, Garrett Horton, so much it hurts. I never stopped. I'm going to tell you those words until the day I die."

"Maybe I'll understand what Jim did when our daughter is born. I'll probably be ten times worse than him."

"Probably." She leaned in and kissed him passionately. "Sunday? I don't even have a dress."

"Come as you are right now. You'll still be the best looking girl in town."

"I hear my parents stirring out there. We better go give them the news."

"Your old man doesn't carry a gun does he?"

"No. But Mom does."

When all was said and done, Big Jim refused to take Garrett's resignation. The only thing that swayed him into staying was Fawn admitting that she'd like to make her life here among both their families and friends. Mining was in her blood too and where better to start a new beginning than among a place they both loved? The mines would be hers someday and together they would decide how best to run them. Fawn had fumed when her father insisted Garrett sign a prenuptial agreement but he quickly signed the paperwork and shoved it at Big Jim.

"There, you hard headed baboon." Garrett snapped. "Happy?" He leaned in and grinned at his future father-in-law. "Because I sure am. If you ever screw with my life again, I will take Fawn to the ends of the earth to avoid her being intimidated and bullied by a father who can't tell his only child how awesome she is." Garrett stood up straight and narrowed his eyes. "Someday you're going to need me, old man."

"When hell freezes over." Big Jim looked over the paperwork Garrett had just signed as if it were a credit card bill. No emotion showed on his face. But as he left, Jim felt a tingling in his left arm. It had been happening more often of late. Sometimes, he got a stiff neck at the most peculiar times. He shook it off and went back to work so as not to have to think about the upcoming wedding.

When Nell found out about the baby, she was at first angry at Big Jim for hiding the information from her.

Next she gave Garrett a "How could you?" lecture, followed by "I love that you're making me a grandmother" speech. Garrett laughed through it all as Fawn looked on in embarrassment. But in true Turnbough fashion, the wedding came off without so much as a hiccup. Money could do that.

They were married, as Garrett wished, after morning services with a packed house to witness the nuptials. Garrett's father was the best man and Garrett's sister, Kathleena drove in to be the maid of honor. Jim insisted he give Fawn away at the ceremony although she at first refused. Only with Garrett's insistence did she relent.

"Thank you, Garrett," Big Jim huffed. "It's a big man who will do that after what you've been through," he said, although he till took no responsibility for the problems he'd caused.

Garrett chuckled with a wicked smirk as he elbowed his future father-in-law. "It gives me great pleasure for you to give Fawn to me in front of God and everybody you know. How does eating that crow taste?" He laughed out loud when Big Jim stormed off to find his daughter.

The reception followed at the mansion where huge tents had been set up for the best food money could buy. The bar-b-que grill fired up with plenty of steaks and chicken for the two hundred people that came to celebrate. An outdoor chef managed the food while a catering company took care of the small details. The local florist, for the first time in her life, wasn't given a budget to make the tables beautiful. Nell's peonies bloomed profusely throughout the grounds. Long rows of colorful iris swayed in beds alongside the walkways that led to Nell's gardens.

It looked as if months of planning had gone into preparing the wedding instead of just a week.

The last of the guests began saying their goodbyes as Nell flopped down in a folding chair and laughed. "I feel like I've been on a roller coaster for the last seven days."

"It was perfect, Nell." Garrett leaned down and kissed the top of her head. "I think I married the wrong girl."

Nell reached out and swatted him on the buttocks. "Get out of here, you rascal." She smiled proudly up at her new son. "I'm so happy I could burst, Garrett Horton. I thought this day would never come."

Garrett looked around to find Fawn laughing with his sister and mother. "Me too, Nell." He looked back down at the woman who was an older version of his new wife. "I want you to know I will always take good care of her. I've loved her since the day she broke her leg riding that fool horse of Jim's."

"And I've thought of you as my own child since that same night you slept on the floor next to her bed in the hospital. I'm so sorry Jim put you through this." She frowned as she watched him approach. "I'm not sure I can ever forgive him."

Garrett chuckled. "Don't be too hard on him, Nell.

Things have always come easy for me, except for having Fawn. This whole episode has made me appreciate what a great life I'm about to have."

"What are you two plotting?" It was Big Jim, a cola in one hand and one more plate of food in the other. "Talking about me?" He sat down next to Nell and took a bite of his sandwich.

"Not everything is about you, Dad." Garrett drew out the word 'dad' with an amused tone.

Big Jim swallowed his food and turned one eye up at him. "Is this what my life is going to be like from now on? One wise ass remark after another?" He started rubbing a spot on his chest then burped. "I think I have a little heartburn." Pushing the plate away, he wrinkled his nose. "Wish everyone would leave so I could take a nap."

Garrett eyed his nemesis with concern. "Heartburn? Since when do you get heartburn?"

"Since about a week ago when you messed up my life," Jim growled.

Nell smacked her husband's arm and winked at Garrett. "He's just teasing, honey. We're both thrilled that we're going to be grandparents. Aren't we, Jim?" When he didn't answer she pinched his arm.

Jim yelped and jerked away before looking up at Garrett. "Just call me Grandpa," he snipped.

Fawn strolled up in her white dress and cowboy boots and leaned into Garrett.

"This is nice, seeing the people I love chatting on a

warm spring day." Fawn touched her father on the shoulder and he grabbed her hand before she could pull away.

"I—" Jim shifted his eyes to Garrett then back to Fawn. "I love you, baby girl. You look so beautiful I can hardly stand it."

"Daddy?" Fawn sounded shocked.

"I'm proud of you for saving that little boy, too." He let go of her hand but she kept it on his shoulder. "It was a fool thing to do, but brave."

"Thank you, Daddy."

She wasn't ready to totally forgive his deception. His actions forced her into a loveless marriage years ago. Thinking that Garrett had betrayed her drove Fawn into other relationships that were destined to fail.

It was only after she returned home to find out Garrett still wanted her that pieces of her heart began to beat again.

Jim waved at all the things that had gone into creating the reception. "Nell, how much is this going to set me back?"

"Not as much as me forgiving you, Jim Turnbough," Nell hissed.

Jim nodded with a smile at his daughter then winked. "I was afraid of that."

Fawn kissed Garrett on the neck and slipped her arm around his waist. "Take me home, husband. I'm anxious to start my new life with the most handsome man in Westfork."

Garrett captured Fawn's mouth and kissed her passionately in front of her parents. "I'm looking forward to other things."

"Humph," Big Jim barked. "Seems to me you've already been doing the 'other things.'"

Nell pinched him again as the newlyweds laughed and took their leave. Big Jim sobered as he rubbed his left arm. "Need any help out here cleaning up?"

"Got it covered, Jim. Go take a nap in your recliner. I think the Cardinals are playing today."

Jim nodded as he stood. The bright sun made him a little dizzy but a big meal would do that to a man. He lumbered into the house and turned back to see Nell giving orders to the crew who would dismantle any evidence of a reception. She wasn't so different from him, he realized. But for right now he needed to rest.

Chapter 16

The moonlight flooded through the windows of the small cabin Garrett and Fawn would call home. The open windows let the cool Ozark breeze drift in the bedroom before tossing the sheer curtains up and down like confused aberrations. The calls of whippoorwills echoed across the woodlands near the creek. The tops of jack pines brushed against each other so often it sounded like whispers floating down from the nearby red bluff that formed one of the boundaries of the property.

As Garrett pulled back the curtain, the moonlight revealed heavy dew glistening on the grass. Closing his eyes, he took a deep breath. For the first time in years, he felt at peace. He looked over at the iron bed to see

Fawn's naked form partially covered by a sheet. Even now as he gazed upon her still body, he could feel his longing stir to life. She would not disappoint him if desire demanded a repeat of their passionate physical need to make up for lost time. Garrett moved to the bed to touch her hair, then her cheek, and lips with his index finger. Sleep was over rated. Something inside him demanded that he keep watch over her, concerned that when he opened his eyes it would have all been a dream.

He slipped in beside her, careful not to cause pain in her injured shoulder. "I love you, Jeanie Fawn."

Even in the darkness, he could see that she smiled. "Show me one more time," she whispered. "Stay with me until we are so exhausted that even the noon day heat won't wake us," she cooed as her hand slipped down to the power that would bring her euphoria. "I need you." Her lips joined his, as the night became the sounds of forgotten love forced to shatter at someone else's hand of betrayal. "Rescue me one more time."

⁂

The newlyweds fell into a normal routine as all couples do. Garrett put in long hours at the Bunker Mine. On those long days, he made sure Nell took Fawn to the mansion to wait for him. Sometimes his new mother-in-law would have saved him a plate food so Fawn wouldn't have to cook. Big Jim would be sitting on the screened in porch reading the sports page of the St. Louis Post or a mining journal. Sometimes he'd come inside to ask Garrett how the Bunker operation was getting along or make a rude comment about it wasn't enough that he took his daughter, now he was having Nell cook for him.

Garrett would laugh and wink at Nell. "The only reason I married your daughter was to get some of Nell's pot roast."

"Humph." would be the extent of the comeback.

"Fawn and I want you to come out to our place Saturday night. We'll grill some steaks. Besides, Jim you haven't even taken a look at that little colt."

Jim frowned but nodded an acceptance. "Nell will bring the dessert."

"No she won't," Garrett argued. He looked at Fawn and smiled. "My wife—" He liked to draw out the word whenever possible. "—will be fixing something and I'll make some homemade ice cream."

Nell hugged her daughter. "Don't overdo it, sweetie."

Fawn kissed her mother on the cheek. "Garrett, did you know I'm the only daughter who has ever had a baby?"

"In that case, we better get you home."

"Need to talk to you first, Garrett." Big Jim didn't ask, just turned and walked back out to the screened in porch. "Sit down." He took up a position at the back of his rocking chair then clamped his large hands on the back. When Garrett remained standing and folded his arms across his chest, Jim realized it was another act of showing disregard for him.

"What is it?" Garrett raised an eyebrow in anticipation of trouble. "Some cry baby says I'm pushing too hard?"

Big Jim smirked, thinking his son-in-law sounded a lot like himself several years ago. "No more than usual." His face turned serious. "I don't trust Charleston."

Garrett unfolded his arms and sat down. "Why? What's happened?"

Big Jim decided he too would sit. He leaned forward with his arms resting on his knees. "I went underground the other day to look at the pillar excavation project and I didn't like what I saw."

"I don't understand. I mapped those pillars out before I left to go to Bunker. It was a safe way to get high-grade lead in the south end. There would be plenty for years ahead if the company needed it. The price of lead has fallen ten cents in the last month. There's no need to take any more of those pillars now. We wouldn't get anything near what they're worth. In two years, prices will be back up and we'll make a killing. Charleston knows this. All the mine supers know it." Garrett's voice had taken on a low, concerned growl.

"Shep Abney put a bug in my ear the other day that Charleston had personally come down and marked some of those pillars. They didn't match the map you left me. I checked them myself. When I ask Charleston about it, he said there must be some mistake. He'd make sure pillar mining stopped until he had some answers."

"So what's the problem?"

"He's lying. I found a memo he sent six weeks ago that estimated the value of those pillars and the prospect of end of year bonuses in that mine. You know as well as I do a lot of people around here depend on those bonuses and I'm glad to give them, but not at the risk of killing someone. If Shep hadn't come forward I still might not know. I think Charleston's looking to impress me. The general manager retires at the end of the year and Charleston is looking to throw his hat into the ring. If he makes a big profit before lead prices go down any further, he'll look like a gutsy visionary."

"That's pretty calculated and risky, Jim. He has too much to lose to try a stunt like that." Garrett didn't like Charleston but couldn't imagine him doing such a foolhearted deception.

Jim took a deep breath, leaned back in his chair, and rocked a few seconds before continuing. "He's afraid of you."

"Me?" Garrett shook his head and grinned. "He's a stupid, petty man that I've tangled with from time to time but I've tried to stay out of his business since I went to Bunker. Running a mine isn't easy, so I've been trying to make amends by keeping my mouth shut, not taunting him." He crossed his legs and propped one elbow on the arm of the chair. "Shep is a good man. He's a good miner and safety is priority one. He's loyal to you and I'm afraid I've tainted his opinion of Charleston. Maybe that's all it is."

"Now that you're my son-in-law, Charleston thinks you're number one on the short list for general manager."

This brought a hearty laugh from Garrett. "Obviously, he doesn't understand our relationship, Jim. Why not tell him you'd rather put that hamburger clown in charge?" Garrett laughed again until he noticed Jim pooch out his lips and rub his chin thoughtfully.

"You're doing a good job, Garrett. I've been grooming you for that job for years. You'd have to screw things up pretty bad to not get it." Jim glared over at the newest member of his family. "Well, say something."

Garrett stood up and turned to leave. "I don't want it."

Jim jumped up and grabbed Garrett by the arm. With a strong jerk, he turned him around to face him. "Why the hell not?" he fumed.

Garrett pushed Jim's hand off his forearm. "Is this another trick to use against me with Fawn?"

Big Jim sighed with disgust. "I know I don't show it but—" He grabbed his left arm and cringed. He turned to sit down and started rocking.

Garrett went pale and came to his side. "Jim, when was the last time you went to the doctor?"

"Don't need a doctor. Just pulled a muscle at work today."

"Like hell you did. How long has that arm been hurting?" Garrett's voice softened. "I need you to take care of yourself, Jim."

"Why is that?" Jim growled.

"I want my kid to know his grandpa." Garrett straightened and watched the old man's lips quiver. He thought he saw something wet at the corner of his eyes but Jim quickly rubbed them away.

"I'll call the doctor tomorrow." Jim had recovered. "Can you help me with this problem?"

"I'll go underground in a couple of days to check it out. In the meantime, I'll talk to Shep and a few of the men I trust. I'll think of a reason to be there. Don't go back down, Jim."

"Humph."

"And go to the doctor." Garrett left the porch and met Fawn outside talking to her mother.

"Everything okay?" It was Nell.

Garrett kissed her on the cheek. "I'm nominating you for the Mother Teresa Award for living with him all these years." He tried hard to sound flippant so they wouldn't suspect his concern over the mine and Big Jim.

෴

That night, as Garrett and Fawn lay wrapped in each

other's arms, the sounds of summer made a symphony outside their bedroom window. The air grew hot and stagnate with each passing day. The window fan soon would not be enough to keep Fawn comfortable. They talked about installing an air conditioner, a better furnace, and adding on a room for the baby.

"Or maybe we could build a new house, Fawn." He kissed her on the temple as he stroked her belly. A sudden kick surprised him as he laughed. "Whoa! That must be the Turnbough side. It was pretty vicious."

"I think that's a good idea."

Garrett laughed at Fawn as he reached over and turned on the light.

"What is it?" She sounded confused.

Garrett folded her back in his arms. "I just wanted to make sure I had the right girl. I expected an argument. I know how much you love this place. But I was thinking we could build a little closer to your folks. That way I wouldn't have to worry when the creek gets up or I'm delayed at the mine. We'll keep this place to bring the kids and tell them how much fun we used to have here."

Fawn snuggled closer. "I like the sound of that. I may need some help, anyway."

Concerned at her tone, Garrett pulled back to look at her. "I knew I should have gone to the doctor with you today." He put his hand on her face and marveled at its softness. "I had a feeling you were holding out on me. What did the doctor say? Is everything all right? I won't miss another appointment, Fawn. What's wrong?" Garrett didn't realize how fast he was talking.

He smirked when Fawn started to laugh and dragged his hand back down to her belly. "Twins. We're having twins. I didn't even tell Momma."

Garrett had twin brothers but never guessed it could happen to him. He blinked and sucked in his breath. "That was some storm we made love in, Jeanie Fawn!" He rolled to his back, smiling from ear to ear. Fawn laid her head on his chest and kissed his nipple. He pulled her on top of him. "Twins. Just when I think I can't get any happier you surprise me." With wild abandonment, he started to kiss her in all the places that brought her to submission.

She closed her eyes and smiled at his fiery touch. "Don't stop," she whispered.

Garrett made the decision the next morning as Fawn scrambled him some eggs and packed his lunch that he wouldn't bring up his uneasiness about her father's health or the problems brewing in the mines. He'd make sure himself that the old man saw a doctor. It would be just like him to use some medical condition to worry Fawn into compromising her pregnancy. In spite of the possibility Big Jim might be showing the first signs of a heart attack, Garrett knew such an event would cause some panic among superstitious miners. Then there was the Charleston matter. After sleeping on the information Jim had given him, Garrett decided not to wait to start his own investigation. He'd start making calls this morning after he'd completed rounds.

The drive over winding roads to Bunker Mine went slower than usual, due to an early morning shower. Slick roads could put a vehicle down a rocky ravine or up a tree if you took a curve at the posted speed limit. Miners considered those numbers a suggestion more than a state law.

Garrett's immediate concern was always the men eight hundred feet below the surface. With a wet spring and early summer rains, the ground grew saturated. A slow summer rain didn't mean there wouldn't be a lightning strike. If the pumps worked, there wasn't a problem. No reports of power failure.

The third shift greeted Garrett as they rose up through the shaft and stepped off the cage into the dim light of a cloudy day. He exchanged a few friendly insults before he walked to his office. He checked the morning reports, called to check on the pumps and daily operations. His mine captain stopped by, informing him of some failed equipment and that the shop was already taking it apart. No delays were expected.

Around noon, he finally had time to make a call to the Rocky Fork Mine. "Shep. Garrett. We need to talk." It would take him about forty minutes to drive into Westfork then another five to reach the mine. Just as he pulled out onto the road, the sky opened up with another heavy downpour.

He thought about calling Fawn. Something inside

him longed to hear her voice. The image of her face made him smile. Even so, the feeling of dread he felt continued to gnaw at him as his truck pulled into the Rocky Fork Mine yard. A shiver ran up his spine as he watched Shep approach. He would later wish he'd made that call.

Chapter 17

The rain slowed as the sun broke through the clouds. Garrett's mother always said if it rained when the sun was out a terrible storm would come later in the day. He just didn't anticipate a mining catastrophe as the storm. The lazy strides of Shep stopped at the cage, holding it for Garrett so they could go down in the mine together. The scowl across his face registered something amiss. Garrett half expected to see Big Jim since he'd left a voicemail before he'd left the Bunker Mine.

Garrett stepped onto the cage then reached for the accordion door. "Where's Big Jim?"

Shep hit the bell cord that signaled the hoist engineer to begin lowering them down the mine shaft. "Already down. Looks like hell. I've never seen him like that."

Garrett stared up at the top of the cage as his fists doubled in irritation. "Crazy old fool," he mumbled. "How long has he been down?"

"Hour maybe. Before you called me, anyway. I went to tell him Charleston gave my crew orders to reclaim some of those biggest pillars in the back. I wanted to go over it with him but he hit the ceiling. Stormed into Charleston's office, only to find out he'd gone underground to check on things. Big Jim took that to mean he'd gone over his head with the pillars and was planning to blast at end of day shift. Said he would take care of it, once and for all. I tried to talk sense into him to let me handle it as long as I had his okay to void Charleston's plan. When I came back with my gear, he'd left."

The cage did a soft bounce as it reached the bottom of the shaft. Both men exited, worried that the boss might physically take Charleston to task. Big Jim, besides being a tall, stout man, could still throw a punch like a sledge hammer.

His temper had dragged him into court on several occasions when he'd laid out a miner sleeping on the job or taking home a few extra tools in a lunchbox. Neither man wanted to deal with another lawsuit on top of everything else going on in their lives.

"Hey, Garrett! What brings you here?" It was one of the electricians.

"Miss you big sissys." The man took the ribbing in

stride with a smirk. "Seen Big Jim?" Garrett asked. "Need to run a few things by him."

"Sure." The man tilted his head down toward the drift or passageway. "Took one of the pickups. Think he's lookin' for Charleston. I know he's your father-in-law and all, but he drove out of here like a bat out of hell. Kept honking the horn all the way down the drift." He laughed. "Maybe he'll be happy when he sees all that lead on the south end."

Garrett looked over at Shep. "What's he talking about? That's supposed to be off limits."

Shep shrugged. "Charleston had me doing grunt work all morning. Been hunkered over crap he usually takes care of. Said I needed the experience. Haven't even looked at the shift foreman's reports. Told Charleston I needed to do that first but he said he'd already done it." His pale brown eyes shifted to the electrician. "Is there another truck available?"

The electrician stuck his fingers in his mouth to create a shrill whistle. He motioned for one of the maintenance men to come then inquired about a truck. Scrambling into one of the small pickups parked twenty feet away, Garrett and Shep went in search of Big Jim before he could get into trouble.

Smells of diesel fuel, wet earth, and rock permeated the air as Shep maneuvered the small truck down the drift. Several times they pulled over to let other equipment pass, slowing them down further. The sound of loaders moving lead to trucks, the thud of rock hitting metal threatened to drown out any kind of conversation. A gesture to turn a certain direction proved to be a better means of communication. The lights grew dimmer as they drove deeper into the drift. The passage gently sloped now as they picked up speed, although that was no more than twenty five miles an hour.

A friendly gesture to acknowledge Garrett's presence from former crew members got nothing more than a nod of recognition as his eyes focused on the cavern opening up ahead. Lights burned brighter there, revealing thirty-foot-wide pillars wrapped in chains. The chains were needed for support, adding a layer of protection in holding up the forty foot high ceiling. Spaced some twenty five to thirty five feet apart, plenty of space remained for Shep to pull alongside the truck that Big Jim drove earlier. A third truck, pointed toward them, idled as if preparing to leave. Two men stood toe to toe, with the larger of the two jabbing a finger in the other's chest.

Two others leaned against the truck observing in amusement, their faces smudged with sweat and hard work, their arms crossed over their chests, enjoying the theater unfolding before their eyes. Until given an all clear, they weren't about to head deeper into the mine to set charges to blast. In spite of being referred to as "powder men," they realized there were just sometimes you didn't play with dynamite.

Garrett and Shep tried to exit the cab of the truck in a

nonchalant manner. Several boulders had been painted with fluorescent yellow paint with the words "Keep Out" and should have deterred investigation. Someone had gone so far as to paint a skull and crossbones on the flag hanging on the cable now laying on the floor of the mine.

"That was up yesterday morning," Shep said under his breath as he and Garrett neared the two men arguing. "I never authorized this, Garrett."

Garrett only nodded, knowing the truth.

Charleston's face twisted with a mixture of anger and fear, but mostly regret. From time to time, he glanced behind him as he shoved his hands onto his waist in what appeared to be apathy. But Garrett knew Charleston well enough to understand confrontation made him uncomfortable. His obsessive, compulsive attention to the details of whatever everyone else worked on made it infinitely easier to either steal an idea or railroad success as the creator.

He was a petty little man with an inflated ego but lacked the backbone of a hard rock miner. Fear shone in his eyes every time he got on the cage then dropped into the mine shaft.

The thought occurred to Garrett that a big score at Turnbough Lead might mean Charleston never had to go underground or at least no more than once or twice a year.

That was why the gutless wonder wanted to harvest pillars.

"You're an idiot," Big Jim roared. "I told you to stay out of here."

Garrett let Shep ease into the conversation as he walked beyond the barricade. Several of the boulders looked as if they'd been pushed aside as easily as moving a child's rubber ball. The big equipment to do this kind of push meant a jumbo had been back drilling holes for dynamite. He could still hear the three men and kept one ear on the conversation.

"Jim, settle down," Shep coaxed.

He wasn't like Garrett, able to demand the old man shut up and listen. Part of him felt a kind of awe mixed with intimidation at being in Big Jim's presence. Shep's father had helped sink the shaft of this mine. It was practically holy ground to his family, including Big Jim, who provided a good living for everyone he ever knew. Shep turned to Charleston. "Did you send my men back there on third shift without telling me?"

"I'm your boss. I don't make my decisions based on your ability to think. You operate with the brains of a possum. The only reason you're the mine captain is because your best friend put you there and Jim doesn't realize his son-in-law is as worthless as they come."

Upon hearing the insult, Garrett looked over his shoulder to see Big Jim rear back with his fist and punch Charleston in the nose, knocking him to the ground. His first impulse was to burst into laughter seeing blood squirt out of the mine superintendent's nose as he struggled to stand. The fleeting thought that his father-in-law had just defended him was quickly circumvented by a faint noise in the distance. He jerked his head around to look back into the darkness where the rubble of several massive pillars lay on the floor.

An image of Fawn in her wedding dress flashed before Garrett's eyes, then her riding a wild horse, followed by her battered body as he pulled her from the school rubble. He heard his mother whisper in his ear to be careful and the cry of babies yet to be born when the hair stood up on the back of his neck.

"Evacuate!" Garrett's body twisted toward the others, his feet already in motion. The three men froze as their eyes caught the look of terror on Garrett's face. "The truck! Everybody!"

Somehow, Garrett reached the truck that was angled to leave first. Snagging Jim's arm as he rushed to open the door, Garrett got the old man's feet moving enough for him to hustle to the passenger side of the two man truck. Shep and Charleston hoped into the seats bolted to the bed of the truck that normally could carry as many as ten miners deeper into the mine.

The two powder men didn't wait to be told twice as they scrambled into the back of the truck.

Although he didn't know the exact danger yet, Big Jim picked up the walkie talkie device and called MineCom to inform them there was a problem. Shep radioed the two blast stations ahead to sound the alarm.

Even before the truck's engine turned over, the glow of flashing red lights in the drift began their ominous signal to escape.

With his hand on the ignition key, Garrett fumbled, managing to grind the starter. The key had been left in the on position, draining the battery.

Nothing.

He pumped the gas then tried again.

"Get us out of here!" Charleston yelled as he grabbed the edge of his seat with both hands. "Hurry it up, Horton."

Big Jim looked over at his son-in-law. "It's dead and we will be too if we don't get out of here. He must have let the battery run down."

Amazed at the calm in the old man's voice, Garrett flung open his door before giving Jim a shove. "Other truck."

Garrett and Jim jumped into the other truck, Garrett behind the wheel, while the others scrambled into the back, banging on the sides that they were secure to go.

The truck fired up but had to maneuver deeper into the mine to turn around. Charleston's truck blocked their passage to safety. Without thinking twice, Garrett yelled out the window. "Hold on!"

Gunning the engine, Garrett plowed into the dead truck moving it enough to slip by and speed down the drift. The truck felt as if it were vibrating just as Garrett realized the ground beneath them shook violently.

Like a child playing with dominoes stacked on end, the pillars began to fall, one by one, slamming into the next, then the next until it created an air blast traveling at the speed of a hurricane.

The mine began to fall apart.

∽∾∽

The construction of the new school was well underway when Fawn drove into Westfork to have a look. It wasn't expected to be ready for the start of the new term. Turnbough Lead brought in enough temporary buildings for most of the elementary classrooms. Before the storm, Jim had purchased a small brick office building off the square that he paid to have refurbished for more classrooms.

The Baptist Church across the street from the school opened up their recreation center for physical education classes.

The school district was in good shape financially, thanks to the lead company's generous contributions. That kind of goodwill went a long way with the people of the community. Turnbough Lead even offered to stock the library with the latest equipment and books needed for young minds.

She met up with a few other teachers for lunch after the tour.

"Any chance the school will hire you back after all

your father has done for the district?" It was a common question.

"I've decided to be a stay at home mom," Fawn said, informing them of the twins.

The conversation quickly turned to babies, a shower, and personal experiences. As she listened to the quiet chatter of her friends, Fawn realized once again how happy she had become in the last few months. What a difference a year makes, she thought. All those years of running from her past, hating the love she couldn't escape and the mistakes she accumulated evaporated the moment Garrett proved his innocence.

Upon separating from her friends at the café, Fawn saw Marcy walking toward her with her head down. "Hello, Marcy." Fawn swallowed hard and tried to be pleasant. "How's my little buddy doing with Rosie the Rodent?" She smiled as Marcy jerked her head up in surprise.

"F—Fawn!" she stuttered. Marcy's body already showed signs of pregnancy. Her eyes darted to Fawn's middle and she quickly diverted her eyes. Fawn, taller and slimmer, could absorb a first pregnancy better than she could. "You look good." Marcy nodded and cleared her throat at the same time. "Joey is much better. I heard you weren't coming back to school. That's too bad."

Fawn didn't quite believe her. "Too many teachers and not enough district money right now. I think I'd like to just be home for a while."

"Not sure I will." Marcy's smile was narrow. "Shep thinks I should but I like having my own money. I think I'll just find a sitter or take the baby with me to work."

Fawn thought taking a little baby into a salon where all kinds of chemicals and sprays were filling a small room would not be the best environment for a newborn. She couldn't imagine Shep going along with that train of thought for his first child.

"I heard your wedding was beautiful. But I knew it would be." Marcy tilted her head and tried not to sound snarky. "Shep wanted me to come but Joey just came home and—"

"You were missed, Marcy." An uncomfortable silence followed until Fawn ventured into dangerous waters. "Look, we're going to be living in the same town for a very long time. Our husbands are best friends. You and I have had some issues in the past, especially the last year. Can we just move past that? If it hadn't been for you telling Garrett about my pregnancy, I'm not sure where I'd be right now." Fawn reached out and touched Marcy's arm. "Thank you." Marcy met her eyes to see if there was mocking. "I really want you to be happy too. Shep is a wonderful man."

For the first time Marcy exhibited a genuine smile. "I bet you were surprised." She laughed a little too loud. "Garrett nearly fell over when Shep told him." She lowered her eyes again in shyness. "I wanted Garrett." Fawn pulled back her hand. "But I need Shep. He loves Joey and me. Garrett never did. He tried, but he just couldn't do it." Marcy stole a look at Fawn who looked as if she would cry.

Fawn took a deep breath. "Do you love Shep?"

Marcy's smile continued. "It's the first time in my life I finally know what love really is and can be. He makes me so happy. With Garrett—" Marcy stopped. "We were really bad for each other, Fawn. If you hadn't come home, the end result would have been the same. It would only have been a matter of time before Garrett left me. I could never measure up. I know that now. He just loved you too much to forget."

"Oh, Marcy," Fawn whispered as she wrapped her arms around the woman who once had been her tormentor. "We've both made so many mistakes in our personal life. Maybe we can start over."

"I'd like that." Marcy took a step back and nodded toward the shop window that displayed the latest baby clothes and crib sets. "I was going to have a look around."

Fawn pulled her purse handle up over her shoulder. "Can I join you?"

Marcy shrugged and smirked. "Let's go spend some money."

A police siren sounded in the distance just as an ambulance sped by them. Fire engines followed. The two women stood still as two more ambulances appeared with flashing lights and sirens. They watched as a half dozen men ran out of the courthouse. Shop keepers and customers eased out onto sidewalks with an uncomfortable curiosity and dread.

Another police car started passed them but pulled alongside a parked car. The officer got out and took long strides back to where the two women stood.

Unconsciously, Fawn and Marcy had hooked arms, clinging tight to each other. They eyed the officer as he approached. His jaw was tight and his eyes squinted as if there was a bright summer sun instead of heavy clouds.

"You Big Jim's daughter?" Fawn swallowed hard and nodded. She felt Marcy's arm go around her waist. "I need you to come with me."

"What is it?" Fawn stood her ground. She felt all those women of the past who'd stood in the expectation of tragedy because they married into the world of mining rally behind her like comforting ghosts.

"You need to come with me. There's been an accident."

Marcy saw the color drain from Fawn's face. "What kind of accident. Is Mr. Turnbough okay?"

The policeman reached for Fawn's arm. "It's the Rocky Fork Mine."

Marcy began to shake. "Shep!"

The policeman pulled Fawn free of Marcy's grasp and starting walking her to his car. "No." Fawn turned back to Marcy. "She comes with me." The officer nodded and the two women slid into the backseat. They grasped each other's hands and both of them stared straight ahead.

"Is there anything we need to do, Officer?" Fawn tried not to let her voice quiver.

"Yes, ma'am. You can pray."

Chapter 18

Blood trickled into Garrett's eyes as he tried to piece together why he lay face down on the earthen floor in a cloud of what felt like dust. His lungs revolted at the sensation of forced to breathe dirty oxygen. Rolling to his back, he took a mental inventory of all his external body parts, hoping nothing had been severed during the gigantic air blast that followed a cave in. All that displaced air had to go somewhere. Every nook and cranny would have felt the blast. Even the shaft would have vibrated with such a vicious push of air. He had a fleeting thought of men trying to escape in a cage just before such an event, which could not possibly end well.

The next sensation was that of darkness so thick it

paralyzed him with fear. Was he dead? Had he been blasted into the arms of hell?

He raised his hands up to find out if he'd been trapped in an air pocket. When his fingers touched nothing, Garrett rose up on one arm and reached higher. Nothing. He felt his hard hat next to him. He flipped on the light at the crown then trembled as he slipped it onto his head. The battery had somehow remained attached to his belt when he'd been thrown from the cab of the truck.

A cough took his breath, forcing his eyes shut against the haze that still managed to sting tears from his eyes.

As he gained control of his lungs, Garrett pulled his shirt up over his mouth to filter the air. Taking his sleeve, he wiped his eyes enough to look around with the beam of light from his hard hat. Something moved next to the truck that had been flipped on its top.

"Shep!" Garrett crawled toward his best friend, feeling gravel on skin where his pants had been shredded in the crash.

Shep tried to pull himself up into a sitting position. His face, a bloody mess, revealed a confused expression as the light hit his eyes. He blocked the light by holding up a hand bathed in blood.

"It's me, buddy." Garrett placed a hand on the man's shoulder. "You look like hell."

Shep grinned as he looked at Garrett's face. "Gotta be prettier than you right now." He too, took inventory of his body. "Nothing seems to be broken but I bet I'm sore as all get out in the morning."

Garrett squeezed Shep's arm in relief.

A groan came from inside the truck.

Garrett fell on his belly to look inside. "It's Jim."

His father-in-law lay on his back, tangled in a rope that had been behind the seat.

The right leg was up over the back of the seat while his left leg bent at the knee. Jim's body pointed toward Garrett. Shattered glass puddled around his head mixed with speckles of blood.

Amazingly enough, the man's hard hat remained on his head.

"Gonna get you out of here, Jim."

The old man turned his head toward Garrett in slow motion, a glazed look of confusion washing over him. He blinked several times before that familiar hard look of omnipotence flooded back into his lined face.

He coughed then tried to move. "Your driving skills stink, Garrett. But what can you expect from someone who learns to drive on a tractor." Jim coughed again and tried to feel his chest.

Garrett chuckled. "Guess that means you're okay."

Jim cringed as he reached a hand back to Garrett who grabbed it firmly. "Kid, don't tell Momma, but I think I'm having a heart attack."

Fawn and Marcy were ushered to an area already blocked off for family members. Someone had been dispatched to pick up Nell Turnbough. She arrived shortly after Fawn, along with other family members of the miners at the Rocky Fork Mine.

Instead of wallowing in her own fear, Nell moved among the group of family members, offering encouragement, ordering others to get a tent set up for a comfort station, and trying to get enough meaningful information to reassure wives and mothers of hard rock miners. This would be what Big Jim expected of his wife, nothing less. When she finally found Fawn standing like the Sentinel of Safety, an award given to mines across the country for no lost-time accidents, she slipped an arm around her daughter's waist.

Fawn leaned over to kiss her mother's temple. "Oh, Mom, I've been terrible to Daddy, these last few weeks. I want to tell him how much I love him."

Strange how a father could morph into a daddy in times of great need or sorrow. Nell reached up with her free hand to pat Fawn's cheek. "He knows that. I know he hasn't told you but he is very proud of you, Garrett too, for that matter. If you didn't stand up to him once in a while, he wouldn't have a lick of respect for you." The sad smile on her face offered reassurance.

One of the geologists came up to offer Nell and Fawn a cold water bottle. "You ladies need to get out of the sun, especially you, Fawn." His head bobbed toward the tent where tables and chairs were being set up.

"Thanks, Johnny." Fawn took the cold bottle and immediately rubbed it against her face. "Has anyone called Garrett? He would want to let his men know. Tell him for me to be careful on those roads if he's coming. Be sure he knows my mom is here with me and that I'm fine."

The geologist went ashen as his eyes darted from Fawn to Nell then over his shoulder at the mine safety supervisor. Without Fawn realizing it, Johnny motioned for the supervisor with the bob of his head. He rushed over to offer support.

"Jeanie Fawn." Nell's arm fell from around her daughter's waist. "What is it, Johnny?" She frowned as she stepped up to him as if shielding her daughter from some awful monster.

"Garrett is already here. He went underground with Shep to find Big Jim. The super is down there too."

A gasp escaped Fawn's lips as her knees began to buckle beneath her. The safety supervisor grabbed her along with Nell.

Her hand went to her stomach as they guided her to the tent then to a folding chair. The news spread like an air blast. Marcy rushed to Fawn's side, pulling up a chair before weaving her fingers through her former enemy's. When their eyes clashed, a flood of tears burst forth as they fell into each other's arms.

In spite of the chaos happening before her eyes, Nell

managed to order someone out to the Horton farm to bring Garrett's parents to the mine. "Do not let them drive themselves," she ordered with a firm tone. Nell then kneeled down in front of both girls and patted their legs. "Now you pull yourselves together. You can pray, wring your hands to blisters, pace, or cuss but you cannot lose hope in front of these families. Do you hear me?" Her look grew stern as she rubbed Fawn's thigh. "You knew the risks marrying a hard rock miner, Fawn. Now pull yourself together. My grandbabies need you to be strong."

Fawn had called earlier in the day to surprise her mother about having twins. She planned to let Garrett tell her father later in the day.

Nell looked at Marcy with a sympathetic eye. "I know all this mining life is new to you, Marcy Ann. I've got no call to order you about, but Shep also needs you to be calm. You want that baby to be strong and healthy. Shep's down there right now worried about getting back to you."

Marcy's tears flowed. "What if he's already dead?" she moaned.

Nell slapped Marcy hard on her thigh, causing her to jump. "Now you shut that kind of talk up right now. It's bad luck."

Marcy took on the look of a scolded child. "Yes, ma'am."

The knees of the older woman popped with arthritis

as she stood up, looking around her at the many concerned faces.

Whispers of terror mingled with the occasional sniffed back tear as ominous storm clouds blocked out the late afternoon sun. The Catholic, Methodist, and Baptist churches had all sent pastors to minister to the hope-impaired families. Food started to arrive even before the tents could be set up to serve.

Nell closed her eyes to say a prayer of thanks that she lived in such a caring community. She felt her daughter stand up to engulf her mother in her arms. "I love you, Mom. Daddy and Garrett are too hard headed to not make it out of this." She hesitated. "Right?"

A nod of agreement helped Nell hold back the damned up tears as she squared her shoulders. "Right."

సమస

The dust began to settle after Garrett and Shep pulled Big Jim from the truck. The area now brightened with head lamps from hard hats. The powder men had been thrown from the truck and, although they had injuries, those weren't life threatening. The men were able to connect their head lamps before beginning the search for Charleston.

"Shep, I know there was a first-aid kit behind the seat. Probably some flares, fire extinguisher, and other stuff to help us out. See if there's a thermal blanket to put on Jim. It's cold down here."

"Looks like Charleston is under the bed of the truck. Not sure if he's alive." It was Tim Setzer, one of the powder guys. He nodded down at Big Jim. "How's he doin'?"

Garrett arched an eyebrow as he kneeled down next to his father-in-law. The man's eyes were closed against the settling dust.

In spite of the open cuts and the dusty patches forming on his face, Garrett realized the old man's skin now was a dangerous shade of gray. He looked back up at Tim, only to shake his head.

"Shep, you're our first-aid guy on the rescue team. Do what you can for Jim. I'll help Setzer and Pyatt with Charleston."

Pyatt was getting down on his stomach to shine a flashlight under the twisted bed. He called out to the mine superintendent then looked at Garrett who squatted next to him. "Nothing. But I think I saw his chest rise. Could have been a shadow."

Standing up, Garrett moved to what was left of the tailgate. "Tim let's see if we can lift this enough so Pyatt can try and pull Charleston out."

Both men were not one hundred percent in the strength department. Each suffered from lacerations, bruises, and probably cracked ribs. The possibility existed that they might have concussions too but, being hard rock miners, they were used to shaking pain and injuries off. They'd worry about that when they saw the sunlight again.

A series of grunts, groans, and cuss words echoed in the mine pocket as the two men tried to lift the backend of the truck.

It wouldn't budge.

"I see him now," called Tim. "He's a mess but breathing."

Garrett came around to his powder man's side and eyed the truck smashed up against the wall of the mine. "Shep?"

Shep stood up from bending over Big Jim. "Washed his face. Gave him some aspirin and water. That should help. He's getting weaker, Garrett. He actually smiled at me."

Pyatt shook his head. "That's not a good sign."

Garrett frowned as he placed his hands on the bottom of the truck bed. "Shep, can you add your back to this and lift? Tim, take that rope over there and slip it around any body part you can reach then pull like hell. If we drop the truck, you won't be under it."

Tim Setzer quickly made a lasso out of the thin rope, which had entangled Big Jim earlier. He nodded to the others as he got back down on his hands and knees. "Okay. Lift," he yelled.

This time, with the extra set of hands, the four men were able to push then tilt the truck toward the mine wall enough so that Tim could slip the lasso over Charleston's twisted ankle. He backed out then started to pull frantically as the others held the truck. A series of painful grunts spewed from the men holding the truck. Arms began to tremble, flexed muscles burned, and veins exposed the amount of strength needed keep the truck from falling on Charleston.

"Got him," yelled Tim as he fell back, exhausted from pulling Charleston's dead weight.

The truck dropped down with a bang, causing the rear tire to blow out. Everyone dropped to the floor of the mine then started to laugh and looked at each other in relief. The two powder men gave a kind of laugh that only men who worked with dynamite could have in the mine. They struggled to their feet, panting, as Shep made his way to Charleston.

After checking him out, he turned to the others. "Looks like he took a pretty good bang to the head. Guess his hat flew off when the air blast hit us."

Pyatt nodded. "We had our hands on top of our hats. Charleston just held onto his seat for dear life."

Another thermal blanket was retrieved from the truck along with someone's lunch box. The contents looked promising—two meatloaf sandwiches, an apple, a couple of cookies, and a thermos of sweet tea. A baggy of homemade granola and raisins had already been opened earlier but enough remained for everyone to have a couple of finger pinches. A gallon of distilled water had sustained a puncture, but had only spilled about a quarter of it into the truck. Everyone took a swig before sitting it in a safe place for later.

Garrett turned toward what should have been their exit. "Let's take a look around, boys."

All four men moved forward to survey the barricade.

"Holy cow. It's a good thing we had to turn the truck around or we would have been at the bottom of that wall of twisted steel."

It was true. Garrett looked at the stacked jumbos, welders, drills fitted together like a macabre jigsaw puzzle. Climbing up onto the carnage, he managed to shine his head lamp through an opening. A forty ton ore truck lay on its side, the top wheels still spinning. He could only imagine how much lead ore was spilled on the other side. The dust floated like a gray curtain on that side of the barricade. The driver probably sustained life-threatening injuries or was thrown under the tumbling lead boulders that flew from the bed.

"Hello! Anybody there?" Garrett's voice echoed in his own ears. He shook his head and called several more times. No light. No activity meant rescue could be a while. He jumped down off the barricade and felt a pain in his lower back. His head hurt but he didn't want to take aspirin in case Big Jim needed more.

"We passed a blast station about twenty feet back. I'll go see if there's anything we can use." It was Shep.

"No. You stay with Big Jim and Charleston." The

mine superintendent started to moan toward gaining consciousness. "I'll go have a look. Pyatt, you get to signaling. Get whatever will hammer a big noise on that jumbo. Can you climb?"

Pyatt grabbed a pipe that had fallen from the ceiling as he nodded acceptance of the job. In moments, the hollow bang of metal to steel pierced the ebb of deadly calm that fell across the mine. Shep began checking vital signs as best he could without equipment, along with making the two injured men comfortable. The second powder man, Setzer, led Garrett back to the blast station to see if anything remained. Nothing did. It was as if some giant had done house cleaning and removed any evidence of the carved-out niche being used for supplies.

Remembering that, when he worked as a mine captain, Garrett had installed metal boxes into the walls of the mines to store emergency walkie talkies, first-aid kits, masks, whistles, and flashlights, he found that something had blown against it, smashing the door latch. In his pants pocket, he reached for the Boy Scout pocket knife he always carried. He kissed the little red knife then opened the blade to pry open the door.

"Eureka." Garrett smiled as he reached in to retrieve the necessities. "I hope these batteries are good. Do you know how long it's been since they were checked?"

Setzer shrugged as he looked back into the drift. "Donno. Let's get out of here. We don't know if more will come down."

Taking a step out, back into the drift, Garrett looked at the wall of fallen lead they'd escaped. His feet made a squishing noise, causing him to turn on one of the flashlights toward the floor. "Water. Pumps are down. That south end can't get rid of it."

"How long we got before it starts coming through that wall?"

Both men started back to the others.

"Maybe twelve hours before we start sloshing around like creek turtles. It's not going to drown us because it'll seep through the jumbo wall ahead. Might get boot deep, maybe higher, but it's sixty-five degrees in here. Won't take long for hyperthermia to set in with us in our current state. Jim and Charleston aren't equipped to survive that. We're going to have to make some kind of platform to keep them up off the floor."

Ordering the banging to stop on the jumbo, Garrett tried using the walkie talkies. He knew what frequency he needed to be on and how to report. He had been practicing this scenario for ten years. The team had taken first at nationals last year then been honored with a banquet upon their return. Then Turnbough Lead had received The Sentinel of Safety Award for the second year in a row for no lost-time accidents. It was a proud day for, not only Jim, but the entire mining community. This meant that safety was priority one. Now it was time to use that training to survive.

Knowing that the rest of the mine rescue team had

already begun to make efforts to find them gave Garrett and the others something to cling to during this lull time. Fear could paralyze them, rendering them helpless in this emergency. It was important to remain calm.

The thought occurred to Garrett that others may be injured or dead on the other side of the wall. How far had the air blast rumbled at speeds of a category 5 hurricane down the drift? Did it take out the cage and hoist? Were men trying to leave at the warning? What Garrett did know was that if they had not taken those extra seconds to turn the truck around, they would all be dead under the piles of equipment twisted into a wall.

"Anybody. Can you hear me?" Garrett frowned as he dropped his hand to his side. With a nod to Pyatt he started hammering again, every thirty seconds or so he would bang his tool against the jumbo.

Garrett looked up at the ceiling some forty feet above his head and thought of Fawn, his unborn babies, and the life they had only just started. Would fate pull another cruel trick on him, snatching the life he craved away from him one final time?

Chapter 19

Darkness began to fall as rescue efforts started to bring up the injured from deep inside the mine. A steady rain began at dusk, making the already-dim prospects of rescue feel more tragic. Men began the arduous trek out of the mine through the escape tunnel around five. Having to climb through darkness after being knocked around like Lincoln logs, took the ten men able to climb the escape ladder nearly two hours. Their bodies, battered from the air blast, weren't as bad as first feared.

Fawn went to the first-aid station to seek out the safety supervisor. The pudgy man's face looked intense as he listened to one of the men from inside the mine give his version of what happened. His weight shifted to one hip as his arms crossed in front of his chest. It was a stance common to miners.

"Mr. Mouser, can you tell me anything?" Fawn was ushered away from the miner on the gurney as a paramedic stepped in to offer the man first aid.

"The mine collapsed at the south end."

"I don't understand. How could that happen? Was there an explosion?"

Having lived her whole life in world of lead mining, Fawn knew enough to know that for a hard rock mine to collapse someone had made mistakes. Lead mining in the Ozarks was a safer place to mine than any other place in the world. They were also the biggest with the highest grade lead.

Mr. Mouser shook his head. "Still getting the info, Miss Fawn. I do know that Big Jim, your husband, and Shep Abney were in the south end." He grabbed at Fawn's arm to steady the trembling. "They said their walkie talkies picked up some static after the collapse like someone was trying to contact them."

"So they could be alive!" Fawn hoped as she placed her hands on the safety inspector's. "When can you go down to see?"

"We gotta get those other twenty miners out from underground. The rescue team is climbing down now to assess what is needed. The hoist man says the cage is a little beat up but when power is restored, we can lower it down the shaft. Others have volunteered to go down and start clearing debris so we can see where the others are."

"Thank you, Mr. Mouser."

"Miss Fawn, we're doing all we can right now."

"I know. I know." She nodded with a forced smile. "Do we know if there are any fatalities?"

"Sorry. I don't know that yet. These guys say there was a crew of thirty today. Ten are now out. Fifteen we know are accounted for waiting for assistance to get out. The powder guys, a truck driver, and of course, the group with your dad, we aren't sure."

Fawn's lips trembled as she pushed her hair behind her ears then laid a hand on her stomach. "It doesn't sound good, does it Mr. Mouser?"

"The guys at the south end probably saved most of these men. They got a warning off in time, Fawn. This could have been a lot worse."

"How long before power is restored?"

"Emergency generators are being installed now. Another hour, maybe a little longer. The rescue team is taking a couple of electrical engineers to get things connected again. Everything has been shut off on this end. If water is coming in we don't want live wires—" He stopped himself from giving too much information as Fawn's face thinned in horror. "This way, we can get the pumps working, too, if they haven't been smashed to hell. Excuse my language, Miss Fawn."

"It's all right, Mr. Mouser. I feel like saying a few rough words myself." She patted his arm. "Keep me posted. Mother is getting tired of comforting others. I'm going to make her sit down a while so I can take over. Please find me if there is any more news." He nodded and started to walk away but she stopped him with a tight grip on his arm. "Good or bad. I want to know."

"Will do, Miss Fawn. You hang in there."

Fawn watched him move to the next man on a gurney, say a few words, then on to the next.

Her eyes fell on a couple of blinking lights outside the mine yard. They were atop a tower that the phone company had just installed for cell phones. The men were not allowed to take them underground because mine captains and safety staff feared a distraction could get someone killed. After several men had taken them, anyway, it was discovered that the lead dust and the cell phones' small computer chips were not a good match.

Fawn caught up with the mine safety supervisor. She tapped him on the shoulder as he moved out into the evening downpour. "Mr. Mouser, I just thought of something." Rain quickly soaked Fawn's hair, dragging the reddish brown strands into her eyes.

The supervisor grabbed her arm and forced her to an awning set up for the mine rescue team. "Miss Fawn, you need to stay out of this rain."

"I know. I'm sorry to bother you. But has anyone tried to call the men on their cell phones?"

The supervisor sighed patiently. "Yes, Miss Fawn. First thing we did."

"Did you try Garrett's? He just got one two days ago." She chuckled, feeling optimism begin to fill in her wounded heart. "You wouldn't have his number."

The supervisor lifted a clipboard then scanned for phone numbers. "Not on here. You got it?"

"Yes. Yes." She took the clipboard and pen, which was tied on with a piece of crochet yard. "Here. He probably forgot to take it out. I nearly washed it in his pants the first night. Had to teach him how to use the stupid thing. The only reason he got one was because of—" She touched her stomach again. "Too much information. Sorry."

"The phone is ringing."

൞൞

Shep cocked his head in response to something that sounded like tin vibrating in a dishpan. "What is that sound?"

Pyatt climbed down off the twisted jumbo. His ears were ringing from the pounding of metal to steel in the desperate plea for rescue.

Garrett heard it this time as he twisted his body around to determine where the sound originated. "There it is again."

They all walked in different directions, thinking they had honed in on the location of the sound. But just as suddenly as it started the vibration stopped.

Garrett lifted one of the walkie talkies. "Hello. Garrett here. Hello."

Static answered with a few garbled words. They let out a yell of enthusiasm.

"Hello. Hello. This is Garrett Horton. We are behind the jumbo barricade." He didn't realize he was yelling. Static answered again but nothing returned this time.

Garrett fought the impulse to heave the small black device at the wall. Then he heard it again, vibrating metal. Moving to the upside down truck and squatting down next to the cab, he listened.

He smiled, tilting his head enough to flood the inside of the vehicle with light. He saw a soft blue light flash then it disappeared under the open door flap of the glove box. Dangerous shards of glass still created a treacherous area for uncovered hands. Garrett took the maintenance manual, which had fallen out onto the torn seat, to use as a broom. Slow to knock away the glass, he wanted to make sure not to throw up a piece that might hit him in the eye or cut a vein. Being methodical meant not taking chances.

Using the manual, he lifted the flap. Lying face down, the smart phone emitted another flash of blue light while emitting the vibration. Anxious to retrieve it, Garrett reached in with his free hand to snatch it.

"Garrett here!"

A shout of hope rolled through the crowd of waiting employees and family members that made up the lead mining community when Mr. Mouser held up the phone to yell, "They're alive!"

Smiles returned to faces that moments earlier looked as if they'd been cast in heavy concrete. Fawn laughed as tears ran down her face. Nell came alongside, drawing her into her arms. She allowed a few tears to squeeze out of the corners of her eyes as she kissed her only child's salty cheeks.

The safety supervisor put the phone back to his ear. Most of the words out of his mouth were things like, "Huh, okay, I see, got it, anything else?" He tried to step away from Fawn and her mother, but several shift foreman and miners took their place.

Everyone held their breath to various degrees. When he clicked off, Mouser stepped into the middle of the onlookers.

Some were wet from standing in the mist now that fell like a warm blanket, others stood with Nell and Fawn to offer support if needed.

Mouser pushed under the awning so that the women could hear. "They're all banged up but alive." A rumble of thanks to God began prematurely. His eyes fell on Nell. "Big Jim may have had a heart attack, Nell." He watched as her hand flew to her mouth. "Charleston is also in bad shape. I think his wife just arrived from St. Louis. I'll talk to her. The others have various injuries."

Marcy Ann came up alongside of Fawn and her mother. "Shep?"

Mouser smiled. "Playing nursemaid to Big Jim and the others. Probably have some funny stories about how the old man was a big baby through it all." His eyes shifted to Nell. "Sorry, Nell. I shouldn't have said that."

With a chuckle, she waved him off. "Don't be silly. Anything else?"

"Just gonna take a while to get to them. The barricade is piled up with lots of loose equipment. There's an air shaft not far from them but it's on the wrong side of the barricade. We could lower some supplies down but we're not sure if they'll be able to make a hole through all that mess to reach it." Mouser heard the hoist start up, drawing his attention in the direction of the cage. "Good sign. We can get more men down to help with clean up now. First, we'll get the ones out that weren't trapped." He patted Nell's shoulder. "Hang in there."

Fawn watched him turn on his heel before walking out into the mist that made the darkness feel thicker. She clung to her mother as Marcy leaned her head on Nell's shoulder then circled the woman's waist with her arm.

"I'm glad they have each other." Nell managed to pat both the girls on their hands. "It will make them stronger." Her head began to bob nervously. "Big Jim will be fine." She sighed. "He's just got to be."

Chapter 20

Looking at the phone, Garrett realized his battery hadn't been charged for the day. He'd meant to plug it in the night before after having dinner with Big Jim and Nell. He'd only remembered this morning as he made coffee. Plugging it in for an hour before heading out the door then again in the truck normally would have been enough. It wasn't like he used it much, or at least not like Fawn who seemed to be constantly scrolling, texting, or checking Facebook. If he knew how to text Fawn he would.

"If I have something to say, I'll call you." That had been Garrett's argument for refusing to let his wife teach him.

"What if I want to just say 'I love you?'" she mused.

"Call me." He'd kissed her on the mouth then slapped her behind. "Besides, I won't be taking the damn thing down in the mine anyway. Rules about that."

Had that conversation occurred this morning? Looking down at his watch to check the time, he discovered the face was smashed. He didn't want to risk using the phone just to check the time so he tucked it inside his pants pocket. At least now, he'd have a link to the outside world. Promising to check in every hour, he realized he would just need to guess about the time.

"You can stop that banging, Pyatt." He motioned for everyone to come closer. "Let's see if we can find a way through that mess." His head jerked toward the twisted pile of equipment. "We might need to put these guys on oxygen before long. The air vent can't be more than ten feet away, probably less."

Shep wiped his sleeve across his face. "That could be tricky. Not sure how secure the other side might be. One false step and it could tumble on top of us."

"We've got to try." Looking down at the two men on the ground, Garrett knew time was of the essence. A moan from Big Jim drew him to the man's side. The thump of his own heart, at seeing the old man so weak, hit a chord deep inside him. Was it fear? If this could happen to Big Jim, it could happen to anyone.

Laying a hand on the man's forehead caused Jim to open his eyes. Bloodshot eyes that watered profusely drove home to Garrett that what he felt was loss. The old man was the worthy opponent who, through deception, hard work, and bullying had forced Garrett into being the man he became for this particular day in time.

"Garrett?" Jim licked his lips as he tried to blink the water pooling at the corners of his eyes. A frown crossed his face as his son-in-law reached down with a finger to remove the wet trail escaping down the side of his face. "Thirsty."

Upon hearing the request, Shep grabbed the gallon of distilled water for Garrett. Slipping an arm under the old man's shoulders, Garrett lifted, feeling the pain in his own body at the strain.

Jim was a big man and dead weight in this condition. Garrett started to offer him the drink when Jim grabbed the gallon jug for himself.

"I'm not dead yet, Garrett. I can do it."

"You're a cantankerous old fool, you know that, Jim?"

"I see you haven't gotten us out of this mess yet." The weak voice tried hard to sound disgusted.

"I keep thinking what would Big Jim do? But then I realized you'd just screw everything up so I'm going to do things my way from now on."

"Garrett, that's enough." Shep kneeled down to help relieve Jim of the jug of water.

Big Jim cut his eyes to Shep then Garrett's solemn face. A smirk played at the corner of his mouth as he doubled a fist then tapped the young engineer on the thigh. "About time. I was beginning to think I had to do everything around here."

The other men chuckled, gaining strength at hearing words from the God of Turnbough Lead stand up to Garrett.

Laying the man back down as gently as possible, Garrett felt Jim slip his hand over his. "How bad is it, boy?"

"They know we're here. Mine rescue is on it, Jim. Things are a mess up ahead of us. Gotta clear it out first. We got plenty of air right now. They'll be pumping more down the air shaft as soon as the power is back on. Can you hang in there?"

Big Jim stuck out his bottom lip. "Bet you didn't think you'd be getting the mines this way."

Garrett squeezed his hand. "Shut up, Jim. Don't tempt me into leaving your sorry ass behind."

Shep cleared his throat then shook his head at Garrett's rough treatment of the boss.

Big Jim smiled and started to laugh but a cough choked him.

Garrett chuckled. "Shep thinks I'm being too rough on you."

"Shep's a wuss." Jim chuckled off handedly, making everyone laugh. Miners didn't mince words in their conversations. He reached over to fist bump Shep's knee then winked. "Best mine captain I ever had."

Garrett snorted. "I resent that." He couldn't contain

his laugh. "After all, I'm the father of your twin grandchildren."

Shock filled Jim's eyes as he looked over at Garrett. His lips trembled as his eyes began blinking rapidly. Shep quickly stood, moving away from the emotional man who was the rock of Turnbough Lead.

"Twins." It was a whisper.

"Twins. Fawn found out yesterday. So you better not die on me, Jim, or I'll never hear the end of it from that spoiled daughter of yours. Damn, she can be a pain in the ass sometimes."

Jim smiled, trying desperately to hold in his emotions. "Like father, like daughter."

"Except for looks. She is hot like Nell."

Jim chuckled again as he laid his hand over his eyes. "Go 'way. I want to rest. Try not to screw anything else up."

It was a spontaneous move on Garrett's part as he bent down and slipped his arms beneath his nemesis, pulling him to his chest. He whispered in Jim's ear. "Hang in there, Jim. I need you."

An arm that once had the strength of a steel beam went around Garrett's back. His voice quivered, but Garrett heard him say, "I love you, boy."

Once Jim was laid back down on the pallet of boards constructed from ones scattered across the mine floor, Garrett turned to the waiting miners with determination. "Let's get out of here."

❧❧❧

Nell had been taken inside the new portable office building with several other women. Cots had been set up for them to get some sleep. Other family members promised to keep a vigil over the miners being brought up from the Rocky Fork Mine. Nell had gone only after Fawn noticed her swaying on her feet. Marcy agreed to take her inside but soon returned to stay with Fawn.

They sat mute, watching activity unfold around them. Ambulance after ambulance arrived, some from as far away as Rolla and Farmington, to help with injured. The Red Cross came late to the scene but, fortunately the community had already stepped up to assist in the needs of the families and friends.

The red strobe lights of emergency vehicles cast an eerie glow over the darkness. Distant thunder rumbled as flashes of heat lighting danced across the Ozark skies. The sound of the hoist lowering men into the mine forced Fawn to hug her chest. The last of the rain dripped from some nearby gutter against a metal bucket that offered a comforting, rhythmic ping.

Garrett's mother sat to one side of her, head bowed, asleep. His father chatted with some of the miners to reassure himself. Sometimes he strolled by, placing his large, rough hands on Fawn's shoulders. No words of encouragement were offered in such a hopeless situation. She knew he didn't understand why anyone would want to go a thousand feet into the earth to dig out the lead that fueled car batteries across the world. She wasn't sure she understood. But it was a life given to her on a silver platter. Now the two men she loved might possibly never return to her unharmed.

She rubbed her belly, mentally speaking to her unborn children. Stories of her childhood raced through her mind—a wild horse ride when she broke her leg, Garrett carrying her to safety, skinny dipping in the Huzzah Creek only to find out Garrett had been watching, and the night he took her body so that she could never love another.

The betrayal of her father had heaped upon her had forced Fawn to run away for ten years, only to return and discover it had all been a lie. Now, with her married to Garrett for such a short time, the world threatened to cave in one more time, denying her the love that had finally rescued her heart.

Mouser returned to squat before her. "Miss Fawn, it's time to call Garrett. Would you like to talk to him this time? Let me catch him up then I'll put you on."

The safety man dialed. "Garrett. Me. Let me talk then you."

Fawn stood, waiting her turn, rubbing nervous hands together as if she were washing them with soap. She sighed as Mouser rattled off needed information for the trapped men then began to listen to the voice on the other end.

"Got someone here to talk to you, Garrett."

Mouser handed the cell phone to Fawn.

"Garrett." Her voice rang out loud in the dark night. "Garrett?" she toned it down.

"How's my best girl?" His voice sounded strong.

"Are you all right? Are you hurt? How's Daddy?"

A laugh came through to her ear. "Fine. No. Bossy. Does that answer your questions?"

Fawn caressed the phone. "Oh, Garrett, I love you so much."

"Love you, too. Always have. Did I ever tell you about the first time I saw you?" Garrett chuckled. Fawn could imagine his laser blue eyes examining her face. "We'd just moved to Westfork. My sister brought you home from school with her to proclaim she had a new best friend."

"I was eight."

"I was ten. I went right out to the barn to find my dad. That's when I told him I was going to marry Fawn Turnbough."

Fawn smiled hoping he could imagine her face. "And twenty years later, here we are."

"Still got the mines coming between us."

The forlorn voice on the other end troubled Fawn. "Don't take chances."

"If I didn't, I would never have won you back." Garrett paused. "Need to save my battery. See you in the light, Fawn."

"I love—"

The line clicked off as she stared at the cell phone then brought it to her chest as if embracing a ghost.

Chapter 21

Wiping the sweat from his brow, Garrett jumped down, nearly falling at the weakness in his legs. "I think we've shored the barricade up enough so we can slip through."

His stumbling forward made Shep step up and catch him. He nodded over at the wrecked truck. "Look who is up?"

Charleston sat against the bed of the overturned truck, pale as a ghost.

"How is he?" Garrett wanted to care but he didn't.

"I think he has a concussion, maybe some internal stuff. No way to tell until we are into the light on top. Both his arms are broken. At least, he can walk out of here if we have to."

"Jim?" Garrett's eyes saw that Big Jim was awake but laying still. Never in his whole life had Garrett ever witnessed the man motionless. Something inside him longed for the foul mouth, disregard for social etiquette, and combative attitude of the owner of Turnbough Lead Company.

Shep shrugged. "I'm thinking another man would be dead. His pulse is weak. Not much we can do but keep him comfortable. If we go through that hole you made, I'm not sure we'll be able to get him to the other side."

Garrett pushed Shep aside with the back of his hand. "Well, I'm sure as hell not leaving him. Jim, do you think if we get you up you can climb up about three feet to an escape hole?"

Jim looked up at Garrett to give a thumbs up.

No argument. No wise cracks. No chastisement of his handling of the situation.

Garrett didn't like it.

Setzer walked up beside him, pointing down the drift toward the cave in. "That water is damming up on the other side. We're coming up on twelve hours down here. Let's face it, even if the power is on those pumps are smashed to bits. Now this place starts filling up with water."

Shallow rivers of water flowed through what had been a safe air pocket.

Garrett's frown intensified. "With this barricade in front of us, the water won't have any place to go. We'll be a swimming pool before long. It probably won't go over our heads, too many leaks on both sides. Hyperthermia is our biggest danger now."

Shep came running up from the back. "Garrett, that water is starting to come in faster. Some of those smaller rocks fell away opening it up. We don't have a lot of time."

Charleston tried to stand on his own but fell back down. Pyatt and Setzer managed to get him to his feet before dragging his unsteady legs toward the opening Garrett had made in the barricade. A lasso slipped over Charleston's head then under his arms as Pyatt scampered up and through the hole, carrying the rope. Together Pyatt and Setzer pushed and pulled Charleston up and through the hole.

Setzer climbed back down to assist Shep and Garrett with the boss. It took all three of them to get him up and moving. By the time they came to the wall, all four men had to stop and rest. They propped Big Jim up against the jagged surface of the barricade as water began to rise, soon reaching the calves of their legs.

"I can't..." Jim put his hand on his heart as he turned his head to Garrett. "Can't do it. Go."

"Shut up, old man. I'm going to get you out of here." Garrett looped the lasso around Jim's chest. "We're going to float you up then push you through the hole. It's not but three or four feet off the ground. Ready?"

The water began rising faster than anyone had expected. Pyatt called from the other side that rescue crews were moving the haul truck and other debris that created the last barricade between them and their air pocket that now threatened to fill with water.

Garrett ordered Setzer through the hole as the water started to float Jim's legs out from under him. "You next, Shep."

Shep shook his head as he pushed Jim up toward the opening. "You're bigger than me. Get up there and get him through the hole. I'll get behind him and shove. Probably going to be the only time I ever get to push him around."

"Funny," Jim responded in a weak voice.

Garrett nodded as he grabbed a hand hold to pull himself up into the opening, making sure he kept a tight grip on the rope. The water rose just short of the opening. It had started finding outlets into their passage of escape.

"I'll pass him down to you two," he called to Pyatt and Setzer who prepared to take possession of Big Jim.

Garrett could see the lights of the big haul truck moving the equipment filling the tunnel beyond. His heart dared to hope they were saved.

"Okay, Shep, on three. One. Two. Three."

Grunts of strength blocked out the yells behind Garrett as he managed to drag his father-in-law through the hole.

A smile of triumph tested fate as he passed Big Jim to waiting hands—more hands besides Pyatt and Setzer's.

He felt his bottom lip tremble as he turned to go back after Shep.

"Shep! Let's go. Need the rope?" Garrett threw it to him before he could answer.

"Nope. I'm good." Shep grabbed a piece of rebar jutting out from the jumbo to pull himself up. When he did, it slipped out, causing the jumbo to tilt, throwing Shep back into the water.

"Get something in here to secure that jumbo. It's falling. Shep is still in there," Garrett yelled to the others.

Climbing back down the barricade Garrett slipped into the water.

Shep was gone.

The muddy water sloshed in Garrett's face as he used his hands to search for his best friend. He heard the jumbo move, yet he couldn't look at the danger while Shep needed him. His legs bumped up against something.

"Shep!" Garrett reached under the water and pulled at Shep's body. Something had pinned his legs. Diving under the water, Garrett shoved at some kind of machine that became buoyant against the last of his brute strength.

Pulling Shep to the surface, Garrett realized he wasn't breathing. He pulled him to his chest as a wail of grief burst from deep inside him but for only a few seconds. It took his remaining strength to haul Shep to the opening where others waited to take his body. Climbing through the hole, Garrett saw that CPR had already begun on his best friend. Water gushed from his mouth but the sight of his twisted leg brought the realization that Shep was in serious trouble. Blood oozed through his clothing suggesting other injuries. Shep's eyes opened momentarily then closed.

༄༅༄

"They're coming up!"

The words spread like wildfire. Television crews had arrived during the night to catch the historic event. Major networks were standing by to get the news in hopes of getting the news first to start out their morning shows. Several helicopters were standing by to transport the last of the trapped miners to hospitals.

Mother Nature appeared to understand that the crisis had been averted as clouds cleared, letting the first rays of dawn warm the wet surfaces so that steam twisted into fog creeping across the yard of Rocky Fork Mine. Hundreds of people gathered, some holding coffee cups and Bibles, others clinging to each other with the hope that all was well.

Fawn and her mother watched as Charleston and Big Jim were carried off on makeshift stretchers that barely fit in the cage. They ran to Big Jim's side, shocked at his frail appearance but thrilled he was alive. Nell held her husband's hand as they moved toward the ambulance, which would take them to a waiting helicopter.

The cage dropped again. Fawn stood rigid, waiting.

The news had not been good about the others. Something had gone wrong. The lines of communication went dark so the wrong information wouldn't get out. She watched as the hoist cables began to shutter, lifting the last of the trapped miners to the surface. Had it always taken so long to rise out of the dark bowels of the earth?

She felt Marcy slip up beside her as the accordion door of the cage was pulled back. Thunderous applause spread across the mine yard as Setzer and Pyatt walked out, bruised and limping. They turned to help someone else.

Garrett stepped out of the cage carrying Shep in his arms like a baby. Water dripped like rain from both of them. Even before Fawn and Marcy began to run, paramedics took Shep from Garrett's arms, placing him on a gurney.

"Hang in there, buddy." Garrett's voice was no more than a whisper as he watched Marcy run to Shep's side, bursting into tears as she fell across his body.

Garrett's blue eyes scanned for Fawn and saw her running to him. As she reached him, he collapsed into her arms and welcomed another kind of darkness to swallow him into relief.

Epilogue

Christmas decorations still filled the hospital on New Year's Eve. Garrett strolled out into the waiting room, pale and exhausted. Big Jim jumped up like he'd been shot out of a cannon as did Garrett's own nervous father. However, Nell and his mother Sarah smiled from ear-to-ear, waiting for the news they longed to hear.

"Two boys." Garrett roared before breaking into laughter. "Fawn is amazing. She must take after you, Nell." He bent down and kissed his mother-in-law then hugged his mother.

The new grandpas grinned before shaking hands.

"Names. What are their names?"

"Jimmy and Jesse, of course." Garrett couldn't resist

thumping both men on the back then pretending to punch each one in the gut.

Big Jim beamed the widest smile Garrett had ever seen on a man. He nodded then turned away, covering up the tears that threatened to spill. He'd become a softy since the mine accident and heart attack. Life appeared to be more precious to him.

"I wanna go back and see my girl," Jim boomed at a passing nurse.

"I don't care what you want," the nurse snapped as she halted her chubby figure in front of them. "The babies are coming into the nursery now. You can go there. But when Mrs. Horton gets into her room she'll need to feed those babies. Then you can come in."

Big Jim frowned but nodded obedience.

The four new grandparents approached the nursery window as if they were sneaking up on a summer snipe in the Ozark Mountains. A lot of cooing, laughter, and compliments flooded the hall between both sets of grandparents. Garrett stood back to soak in the warm glow of the moment.

A year earlier he hadn't imagined this scene would ever come to pass. Now here he was, father of two and married to the most wonderful woman in the world.

Garrett's head turned as the elevator doors chimed and a wheelchair pushed out with a man cradling a baby wrapped in a pink blanket. A woman pushed him out then waved to him.

"Shep! Should you be out with that baby girl of yours?"

"He wanted to be here for the happy occasion, Garrett." Marcy reached down to pull back the blanket from her month old baby girl. "So boys or girls?"

"Boys. Jimmy and Jesse."

"How's the leg, buddy?" Garrett wasn't sure if the doctors would be able to save it after being crushed under the equipment during the cave in. But the water had kept it from pinning him down too long when Garrett reached him. Others said Shep had drowned and, thanks to Garrett's quick thinking, he was revived in time.

Shep gave a grin as he shook Garrett's hand. "My leg will be good enough to kick your boys to kingdom come if they come hound doggin' around my little girl. Just remember she's got a big brother too."

Garrett laughed. "I'll be sure to keep that in mind, Shep."

Nell walked over to take a peek at the newest baby girl in their circle before looking at Garrett. "Sweetie, they're taking the boys back to Fawn. She wants you there."

Garrett ran to Fawn's room, loving how it had felt to hear Nell say "The boys."

He was a father. His heart beat so hard he had to stop outside the door of Fawn's room and catch his breath.

As he pushed open the door, he saw Fawn sitting up in bed, nursing one of the boys. Her reddish brown hair had been pulled up in a ponytail, making her look younger.

"Come meet your boys, Garrett," she said. He sat on the bed and touched the little head that fed at his mother's breast. "This is Jesse," she told him, kissing the one she was holding. "Can you pick up Jimmy for me?"

Bringing his other son over to join them, Garrett locked eyes with Fawn in a bond that neither had imagined possible in all those lost years apart.

Garrett kissed his son then Fawn's lips. "Fawn, thank you for loving me, believing in me, and giving me a second chance."

She swaddled the child in her arms then leaned back against the pillows. "I'm glad you didn't give up on me."

Garrett offered a wolfish smile. "You know I'm going to want a little girl now, right?"

The moments of new-found joy began to flow into a life together that would be awash with more children, mining exploration, and growth in the empire that became known as Turnbough Lead Company and Sons.

THE END

About the Author

Tierney James has been in education for over thirty years. She currently teaches World Geography for a nearby college. Besides serving as a Solar System Ambassador for NASA's Jet Propulsion Lab and attending Space Camp for Educators, James has traveled the world. From the Great Wall of China to floating the Okavango Delta of Botswana, Africa, she ties her unique experiences into other writing projects such as the action thriller novel, *An Unlikely Hero*. Living on a Native American reservation and in a mining town for many years, fuels the kind of characters she never tires of creating. By taking readers into the depths of the earth, James hopes her novel, *The Rescued Heart,* will show the courage and dangers of loving a hard rock miner.

With teaching college classes and writing workshops, James also enjoys gardening and reading. Other pursuits involve learning Hebrew and research, which sometimes has led to becoming certified with various weapons. There's never a dull moment in her life. And that is just the way she likes it.